Arthur Wood

Shoddy - A Yorkshire Tale of Rome

Vol. III

Arthur Wood

Shoddy - A Yorkshire Tale of Rome
Vol. III

ISBN/EAN: 9783337121617

Printed in Europe, USA, Canada, Australia, Japan

Cover: Foto ©Andreas Hilbeck / pixelio.de

More available books at **www.hansebooks.com**

"SHODDY."

A Yorkshire Tale of Home.

BY

ARTHUR WOOD.

IN THREE VOLUMES.

VOL. III.

LONDON:

TINSLEY BROTHERS, 8, CATHERINE STREET, STRAND.

1877.

[Right of Translation reserved by the Author.]

LONDON:
SAVILL, EDWARDS AND CO., PRINTERS, CHANDOS STREET,
COVENT GARDEN.

CONTENTS

OF

THE THIRD VOLUME.

———

"SHODDY."

CHAPTER I.

OFF DUTY.

DOUBTLESS there are many persons living now, who can remember that period in the history of art in this country, before M. Daguerre had dealt the death blow to miniature painting by his ingenious process of photographic portraits, when a speaking likeness was, by persons of an imaginative turn, supposed to be obtained by cutting out a profile in black paper. This branch of art obtained much favour at one time, and there were few families of any position at all who could not boast among the reminiscences of home one or more irregular blots, which, framed and hung against the wall, served to remind an affectionate posterity of some deceased relative, whose prominent nose, protuberant forehead, or facial angle, more or less obtuse, was faithfully reproduced by the cunning scissors of the artist. For

myself, I have ever regarded the *silhouette* portrait
as a deception practised upon a guileless and cre-
dulous community; and excepting such instances
where the original had some abnormal character of
profile or striking eccentricity of costume, quite as
suggestive of the entire species as of the individual.
So, as being the kind of portrait very much in
favour at the time, and as pleasant reminders of
days long past, and of many happy years of married
life, a *silhouette* profile adorned each side of the
fireplace in the cosy breakfast parlour of Mr.
Titheradge's comfortable residence, that looked
over Streatham Common.   I am compelled to
admit, in the interests of truth, that but for the
black splashes and knobs that represented the
huge cap and ribbons of Mr. Titheradge's faithful
partner, and the blank space left by the skilful
artist on the white card, to denote the old-fashioned
white neckcloth and collar that Mr. Titheradge
habitually wore, you might, as far as any likeness
went, have gazed on the lady's portrait and
said, " How like my old friend T. to be sure !"
or examined his profile and remarked, " Mrs.
Titheradge some years ago, I observe," and
yet have been not more in error, than those very
shrewd observers of character who, after a business
interview with the old and sagacious lawyer in his
chambers, came away with the conviction that he

was only a keen man of business, or even a "sharp practitioner," with as much heart as the often-quoted paving-stone; and if, as we have the authority of antiquity for believing, the bowels are the dwelling-place for the tender sentiments of sympathy and compassion, that in his case either the property was not tenantable, or the occupants had been removed by some writ of ejectment.

In both cases I draw this inference, that for a faithful portrait, or correct estimate of character, we should avoid painting our subject in black, and contemplating it only when so depicted, as a good many lights may be obscured by the heavy colouring, which would otherwise give much life and point to various dimples and curves, and without which the picture is imperfect. Thus, if those keen observers of human nature referred to could have seen the astute old lawyer in his garden before breakfast, on a fine spring morning, and with hoe or rake in hand grubbing up the weeds, or removing the stones, wearing a straw hat and an old shooting-jacket, and sometimes in the evening with the addition of a long clay pipe, they would scarcely have believed him to be identical with the staid gentleman who, in his suit of black and white neckcloth, left his gate at precisely nine o'clock to catch the omnibus that should take him to town.

And this was the surprise that awaited his young student, Mr. Frank Ossett, when, after excusing himself from many invitations by Mr. Titheradge to dinner, from a misgiving of an evening of utter dullness and boredom, he at last, for very shame, consented to accompany him to Streatham. He found how unfairly he had judged the old gentleman in contemplating his character from the *silhouette* point of view only.

It was a bright and genial afternoon in May, and seated on the outside of the omnibus, Frank enjoyed his ride extremely. It might be that Mr. Titheradge was also exhilarated by the fineness of the day, and that as he left the smoky and noisy city, the soft south wind from the Surrey hills blew back the sordid cares and anxieties of life to the wilderness of brick and mortar behind them; but it is certain his young companion was first astonished, and then charmed, by the freshness and geniality that he never suspected lay within that formal outline of a mere man of business.

At the termination of the journey, the old gentleman alighted with a good deal of agility, declining Frank's proffered assistance, and swinging himself to the ground with the dexterity of a young and active man.

" Now, Mr. Ossett," said he, " we have only a

ten minutes' walk before us; but I always have a glass of ale at this house—will you have one? It's the best I get anywhere. Do as you like, of course, but so must I."

Whereupon with a jaunty step, and humming a little tune, he led the way to an old-fashioned looking hostelry by the roadside.

"By Jove!" Frank said to himself as he followed, "what a fine old fellow this is going to be! I am deuced glad I came!"

The landlady behind the bar received Mr. Titheradge as an old customer, laughing readily at his jokes, and merrily saying, "As before, sir?" at once drew the ale, and offered a snuff-box, which she took from a shelf behind her.

"I don't take snuff as a rule, Mr. Ossett," he said; "but a pinch now and then—Ha!"

"Will you walk into the parlour, sir?" the landlady said.

"No, bless you, no!" he replied. "What would my good lady say? As our friend John Gilpin has it, 'The dinner waits and we are tired, says Gilpin, So am I.' No, no! Good day—good day."

"That house has a sporting look about it, I think," Frank said, becoming every minute more at ease with his companion. "I saw a portrait there of a fighting-man."

"Oh, ah!" Mr. Titheradge answered. "To be

sure—Tom Spring (his proper name was Winter, by the way). Ah, a fine fellow that! I saw him fight Langan—an Irishman—at Worcester, many years ago."

" God bless me !" Frank cried, standing still for a moment to stare at his companion. " You don't say so !"

" What's the matter ?" Mr. Titheradge asked quietly.

" I had no idea—I mean to say I shouldn't have thought you would have cared about that kind of thing, sir," Frank said.

" Well," said the old gentleman, laughing a little, and in perhaps a slightly deprecatory tone, " it was the fashion then, and I was a young man, you know."

" Then," Frank asked, with some animation of manner, " you don't altogether disapprove of it ?"

" Well—eh ?" Mr. Titheradge rejoined, " you see, times are changed now; but perhaps as our friend Sir Roger de Coverley said, when he was pressed for an opinion in his magisterial capacity, ' There's a good deal to be said on both sides'—eh ? But one moment; here is some one I want to speak to, if you'll excuse me."

Frank, looking up, saw approaching a low pony-phaeton, and as Mr. Titheradge crossed to the other side of the road to speak to a gentleman who was driving, Frank walked slowly on, merely observing that the other occupant of the vehicle was a lady, and from the cushions against which she leaned, and a heavy veil she wore, he inferred her to be an invalid.

"Friends of ours," Mr. Titheradge said, when he rejoined Frank. "The lady has been ill. Mrs. Titheradge takes great interest in her—in fact, she makes a sort of cade of her. You see, we have no children of our own, that is, living—living; and Mrs. Titheradge is one of those women who must have a pet of some kind."

They walked a little way in silence, for Mr. Titheradge had become suddenly grave, and more like his other professional self, and Frank, on whom his last words had made some impression, began to have forebodings that his prospective enjoyment would, after all, be baulked by the mistress of the house, of whom he conjured up imaginary pictures. He thought of all the disagreeable old women he had known, and was wondering which she would most resemble, when he was startled by Mr. Titheradge suddenly opening a garden gate and saying—

"Here we are, then."

A small, comfortable, double-fronted house of red brick, and two stories high, in a garden kept with scrupulous neatness, and amid a profusion of

plants and flowers. The door was opened by a
trim servant girl, and a pleasant odour, indicative
of approaching dinner, found its way into the hall.
Her mistress, the girl said, in answer to Mr.
Titheradge, was in the back garden.

" Come, then," said Mr. Titheradge, " we'll join
her there." It was a large plot of ground, every
available foot of which was carefully cultivated, and
quite as trim as the one in front, but with a view
to utility instead of ornament. Fruit trees were
carefully trained and nailed on the southern and
western sides of the walls, with beds well stocked,
and each with a stick and a label attached, describing
the crop and the date of planting, and a pleasant
little greenhouse on the sunny side of the house.
They found the mistress of the house, attired in a
garden apron and a large hat and gloves, placing
some soot and ashes at the roots of the fruit
trees.

She met Frank with an old-fashioned salutation,
half bow and half curtsey, and taking off her garden
gloves, welcomed him cordially. She was a larger
person than Mr. Titheradge, with a round, good-
humoured, red face, and a not unpleasant bluntness
of speech and manner.

There was something so unpretentious, almost
homely in the manner of his host and hostess, that
Frank was hardly prepared for the admirably

appointed dinner that was announced shortly afterwards. The dining-room was small, but luxuriously furnished; the dinner perfectly cooked, and with appropriate wines for each course; and yet everything was served so quietly and with such precision, that Frank had a conviction this was the rule of the house, and not an exception in his favour. The dear old lady at the head of the table talked away pleasantly, telling her husband the little news of home, and interesting him in the progress of his garden crops, breaking off now and then, to assure Mr. Frank she was glad to see him, or to say she had the pleasure of knowing both his parents and hoped they were well; but her voice was not a loud one, and though she was somewhat liberal in the application of her H's, and appeared rather indifferent to some of the subtleties of grammar, it was impossible, Frank thought, to look on her genial and kind face and dwell on such trifling inaccuracies.

You see, thorough kindness of heart has a charm of its own. It has a marvellous power of lighting up an otherwise dull face. Under its benign influence plain persons are attractive, and we do not care to remark the defects of the unlearned. Perhaps it does not impart that fire to the eye, and that thoughtful grandeur to the features, which, I believe, it is the province of excessive intellectuality to convey; but probably it has a compensating quality of its own, for in its presence the timid recover their confidence, shy persons forget to be embarrassed, and it never calls for that antagonistic and watchful spirit, which in self-defence most of us have experienced, I doubt not, when in the privileged presence of that mental superiority, which, we know, may at any moment think proper to humiliate us.

Perhaps Mr. Frank Ossett had some such reflections, for he was conscious he had been silent some time, leaving his entertainers to do all the talking, so rousing himself, he made some observation of a professional nature to Mr. Titheradge; but that gentleman, becoming instantaneously the Titheradge of Titheradge and Burnley, solicitors, replied, drily, that at that moment he was not prepared to say, and immediately turned the conversation to other subjects.

Later on, Frank incautiously asked another question bearing directly on legal matters, and, as drily as before, Mr. Titheradge was not prepared to say; but if Mr. Ossett would remind him to-morrow at chambers (slightly emphasising the locality), he would go fully into the question.

So Mr. Frank, who was by no means the keenest observer of mankind, was compelled to recognise how entirely all business matters were

to be ignored in the presence of Titheradge, solicitor, Raymond's Buildings, when out of business
hours.

"That's the picture of a good cob you have
there," Frank said, noticing an oil painting of a
stout, little dappled bay, with saddle and bridle;
"an old servant of yours, I presume?"

"Servant, Mr. Ossett?" the old gentleman said.
"An old friend, sir—an old friend. We were
companions, sir, for twenty years. I bought him
when he was rising five. He carried me for
twenty years, and never made a mistake. He
couldn't make a mistake, sir! He didn't know
how. It was the only thing that pony couldn't
do. Then his feet failed him, poor fellow, and I
never worked him afterwards."

"He looks the right sort," Frank said, with the
admiration which the inherent love of horses, common to Yorkshiremen and all good fellows, aroused.
"Is he still alive, sir?"

"No," said the old gentleman, softly. "He's
dead, sir—dead."

Speaking of this afterwards, Frank declared that
the old fellow's eyes filled with tears at the mention of his dead favourite, and always grew angry if
his own statement was doubted, or Mr. Titheradge's emotion ridiculed.

"He was a great cade, Mr. Ossett," the lady

said; " and if I went into the paddock—for we didn't live here then—and called ' Dapple, Dapple,' he would trot up to me like a dog—aye, better than any dog—and nuzzle about with his nose till I gave him an apple or bit of bread. And as for poor dear Carrie—that was our daughter, Mr. Ossett—Mr. Titheradge bought Dapple for her, as the doctor recommended 'orse exercise for her— poor dear! (in 'eaven now, Mr. Ossett); he was as gentle with her as a lamb, as if he knew she wasn't long for this world as well as any Christian."

" I think," Mr. Titheradge said, quite gravely, " if perfect fidelity, gentleness, and patient endurrance may be taken into account, Dapple was better than most Christians I have had the privilege of meeting. Give Mr. Ossett a glass of that champagne," he said to the servant, as if desirous of changing the conversation. " I think you will like that, sir; it's a nice dry wine."

While they were seated over their dessert, the noise of carriage wheels was heard, and Mrs. Titheradge saying—

" Oh, my dear, they have returned — if you will excuse me," rose to leave the table.

Mr. Titheradge said " Certainly," and also rose to open the door for his wife, making a stately little bow as she passed out. As the carriage was driven away by the groom, who had been waiting

for the purpose, Frank fancied he recognised in
the grey horse and the low build of the vehicle, the
phaeton he and Mr. Titheradge had met on their
way to the house.

" Now, Mr. Ossett," said his host, when they
had been left alone a little while, " I hope you will
help yourself and do as you like ; but for my part
I enjoy a pipe in the garden on a fine evening like
this. What do you say ?"

Frank assured him nothing could be better to
his own taste.

" Then kindly touch that bell behind you there—
and ring twice; that saves trouble."

The trim little servant understood the signal.
It was manifestly an established custom, for without further directions she brought a tray with a
box of cigars, and some pipes, long and large in
the bowl, one of which, very much discoloured by
use, Mr. Titheradge selected. Frank took a cigar,
and his host, pausing for a few seconds in the hall
to put on an old felt hat, and to exchange his black
coat for an old well-worn, plaid shooting-jacket,
led the way to the garden at the rear of the house.
They strolled about the paths for nearly an hour,
in the lovely twilight of the spring evening, conver-
sing on a variety of subjects—always excepting
those that had reference to business—and had been
admiring the promising show of a large strawberry

bed, loaded with its delicate white blossom, when
Mr. Titheradge said, quietly—

" Stand perfectly still for a moment, Mr. Ossett.
Don't step back, or you will hurt the little
Emperor."

" Hurt who ?" Frank asked.

" No ; all right ! Step forward—yes, that's it !"
Mr. Titheradge said.

Frank, turning to see who the little Emperor
might be, saw a large toad, squatting in the garden
path.

" Yes," Mr. Titheradge said, " I call him the
Emperor, in remembrance of—who was it ?—Domi-
tian, I think, who relieved the monotony of life
by killing flies. So does our little friend there
with the bright eyes ; and, I think, of the two, he
is the more estimable character. Hush !" he continued, laying the bowl of his pipe on Frank's arm
to secure attention ; " did you hear ?"

" What ?" Frank asked.

" No," the old gentleman said ; " I was mis-
taken. I thought it was the nightingale ; we hear
him sometimes, but that is the note of the thrush ;
quite as beautiful, to my thinking, if he only had
the *nous* of the other."

" Eh !" Frank cried, laughing.

" ' Sweet Philomel,' as our friend Milton has it,"
Mr. Titheradge said, " knows the valve of mono-

poly, and sings at night when the others are silent. Perhaps, in a Competitive Examination he might not be so successful. But I think we are too soon for him at present."

Just then the servant approached to announce coffee, and they returned to the drawing-room, Mr. Titheradge again staying in the hall to divest himself of his old hat and jacket, and to resume his black coat.

Frank observed the same comfort and luxury that had marked the other parts of the snug little house. Without possessing much critical capacity for works of art, he seemed to feel that the engravings and water-colour drawings on the wall were rare and valuable. A piano stood open on one side of the room, and a trio of clarionettes reclined in an angle of the wall near it.

"Well," Mr. Titheradge said, as he entered the room, "how's—how's the patient?"

"Better, I think, this evening, and stronger," his wife replied.

"A young friend of ours," Mr. Titheradge explained, "has been an invalid, and is staying with us for change of air. Are you at all musical?" he asked, seeing Frank's attention directed towards the open piano.

"No," the young man said, in a tone of regret, "I am sorry to say I am not; but I was just won-

dering who would be the performer on the clarionettes there."

"Oh!" said the old gentleman, " I am the performer.   Yes, it is a favourite instument of mine,
though I never play now."

" Ah, I wish he would," the lady said ; " he
used to play beautiful once."

" Well," Mr. Titheradge said, with a not unpleasant self-complacency, " I used to fancy myself
a little on my A flat."

" Dear me !" Frank cried, in simple astonishment, " how surprised I am !"

" Indeed !" the other rejoined, smiling ; " and
why ?"

" Well, sir, pray don't think me rude or impertinent," Frank said modestly ; " but it seems to
me so strange, and yet so delightful, that a gentleman of your strict business habits, and standing so
high—may I say ?—in your profession, should have
the faculty of entirely leaving behind him in his
office all the cares and harass of business, to enter
upon, as it seems to me, quite another' kind of
existence at home, and which, I must take the
liberty of saying, seems perfect domestic happiness.
I am afraid," Frank continued, reddening a little,
and bowing to Mrs. Titheradge, " it may sound
unbecoming in me to venture such an observation,
but I assure you, ma'am, it has been wrung out

of me by the very delightful evening I have passed."

"My young friend," Mr. Titheradge said, laying his hand kindly on the lad's shoulder, "whatever you do in this world, give your mind to it. Failures in life result quite as much from indecision of character as from want of capacity. Having once made up your mind, concentrate your will. In the hour set apart for work, let no other thoughts distract you—you will enjoy your leisure all the more ; and, on the other hand, let your leisure be your leisure. The difficulties of to-morrow will be met by to-morrow's efforts. The work which, at your age, I did not like, has become a necessity for me now, and I should not be well without it ; for, after all, we are only creatures of habit. When I am no longer fit for my trade, as a scavenger in the dusty roads of the law, I shall no longer be able to smoke my pipe, trim my flowers, or blow my clarionette ; and, Mrs. T., my dear, you may then consult your milliner on the most becoming fancy in widow's weeds, for you may make up your mind you would shortly have to wear them."

"Really, Titheradge, how can you !" the lady exclaimed ; "you ought to be ashamed of yourself, talking in that way !"

And the comely round face assumed the only melancholy expression Frank saw it wear that evening,

But the conversation soon took a more lively tone; and shortly afterwards Frank, noting the time, rose to leave.

The farewell of the old people was as hearty as their greeting had been; and his host, regretting he could not offer him a bed, as their only spare room was occupied by their young invalid friend, accompanied him to the outer gate, shaking hands cordially when they parted.

Ten or twelve minutes' brisk walking brought Frank to the door of the tavern, from which the last omnibus to town was about to start.

The conductor was seated on the little step by the door, and observing Frank said—

" Last 'bus, sir !—going to town, sir ? Start in two minutes."

" I suppose you will have time for a glass before we go ?" Frank asked in turn, feeling extremely well-disposed towards every soul in the universe.

" Thank you, sir," the man said ; " we shall have time for that if we're sharp. This way, sir ?"

As he seemed to know the house, Frank was quite content to accept him as guide, and followed him into a portion of the bar marked private. Here they found the driver of the omnibus drinking spirits, to whom the conductor introduced Frank as " a gent going up."

"All right, sir," said the driver; "room on box seat. Nice night for a smoke;" and immediately drained his glass, timing it so skilfully as to place it down empty as Frank was ordering something to drink for the other man. Seeing this, the young fellow invited him to join them; which proposal, it is perhaps needless to say, was instantly acceded to. The usual two minutes before an omnibus starts having expanded into the customary ten, and several passengers having lodged their angry protests against any further delay, the lad mounted the seat beside the driver, and they started homewards.

Frank, delighted with the unexpectedly agreeable evening he had passed, and in good humour with himself and everybody else, was, as the driver afterwards remarked, "that affable," that he, in his turn, was also extremely communicative. So, after a few observations on indifferent subjects, Frank said to the driver—

"Do you happen to know a gentleman named Titheradge? Lives on the common there; comes to town every morning."

"Can't say as I do by name," the man replied. "What's he like?"

Frank was proceeding to describe Mr. Titheradge's appearance when the driver interrupted him with—

"Oh, him ! Oh, ah, I knows him fast enough. Goes up by the nine fifteen 'bus regular. Good as a clock to go by. Something in the City, I think."

"Lawyer," Frank said.

"Ah, just so ; always gets down at the Cross," the other said. "Lots of money, I hear—married his cook, I'm told."

"Married his cook !" Frank exclaimed. "Why how in the world do you know that ?"

"Don't know, I'm sure," the driver said. "Heerd a gent say so one day. George !" he cried, turning half round to call to his conductor, "didn't we hear as the old gent in the white choker, as goes up by the nine fifteen, married his cook ?"

"Ah," the conductor said, indifferently, "there or thereabouts."

There was little enough in it—this gossip on the road—but it set the young fellow thinking, and very hard.

"Ah," he thought, "she did knock the H's about a little, and didn't always speak the best grammar; but cook or no cook, she's a dear good old soul, and like mother about the eyes when she smiles."

He lighted a cigar, and offered another to the driver, which that worthy was far too well-bred to pain Frank by refusing. He also endeavoured to beguile the tedium of the journey by observations to Frank on the questions of the day, and by occasional sallies of satirical wit against persons whom they met or overtook on the way, assuring him, if there was one thing more than another he enjoyed, it was a pleasant weed on the box, and a friendly chat with a gent as knowed his way about, which it might be you, sir.

Feeling somewhat chilly with his ride in the night air, Frank left the omnibus at Charing Cross, for the purpose of walking through the Hay-market and Regent Street on his way home. He had paused for a few minutes at Oxford Circus, undecided as to the nearest way when a gen-tleman, who was walking with a hurried step to-wards the West end, said to him in a tone which seemed familiar—

"Oh, could you tell me, am I in the right direction for the Hampstead Road?"

"Hampstead Road!" Frank cried, "why you are walking away from it. But I say, wait a moment," he added, moving so that the light from a lamp might fall on the other's face; "Yes, it is Mr. Palethorpe from Dalesford, surely!"

"Yes, indeed—why I declare!" the Reverend Ernest exclaimed. "It is Mr. Ossett!—well, really!"

I believe if there were one man in the world for whom Frank had a sincere aversion, it was the estimable young curate then standing before him. But he was too happy himself to allow any feeling of animosity to exist; and he said, as he shook the Reverend Ernest's cold and damp hand—

"Good gracious! what are you doing here at this time of night?"

"Well," said the Reverend Palethorpe, simpering; "I am in a little difficulty. I came up to day, by my Rector's kind concurrence, to attend a few meetings, and by the recommendation of a friend— a Christian lady friend—I went to an address in the Hampstead Road. I have taken a wrong turn, I suppose, and had lost my way."

Frank telling him he had a long way to walk, and being a stranger in London, might have some difficulty in finding it, advised him to call a cab. But as the Reverend Ernest had neglected to take the number of the house where he had proposed to sojourn, there was another difficulty.

"But," said he, "if I can find the Hampstead Road I dare say I shall manage very well; for though I have forgotten the number, I think the name of the person who keeps the house is Wright, or Knight, or some name very like it."

"If you have no better clue than that, its a poor lookout at this time of night," Frank said.

" However, you can tell the cabman to drive you to Hampstead Road corner—it wont be more than a shilling or eighteenpence fare ; and if you think you can remember the house, that will be a lift on the way."

" Well—yes ; thank you very much," Ernest said, simpering ; " but the fact is, I am in another difficulty. I have had the misfortune to have my pocket picked."

" The deuce you have ! Where ?" Frank asked, bluntly.

" Well, I don't exactly know," the Reverend Ernest said, with some hesitation ; " but I think it must have been in an omnibus."

" Oh !" Frank said, feeling some difficulty at refraining from laughing, though he did not quite know why. " Very likely in the omnibus. ' Beware of pickpockets—male and female.' Just so. Well," he continued, looking at his watch, " it isn't much past eleven ; you can't walk about London streets all night. Come home with me ; I live not far off—in Seymour Street. You can have some supper, and perhaps my landlady—she's a good sort of woman—will extemporise a bed for you."

" Well, really, Mr. Ossett," the curate replied, " under the circumstances, I shall not say no. It is not at all a bad idea."

Frank selected a two-wheeled cab, with a horse whose blood-like head suggested a broken-down racer perhaps—whose palmy days of heath and downs had long since vanished, like those of the spirited sportsmen probably who had rashly put their money on him—and he whisked them along at a rare speed. So satisfied was Mr. Ossett with his choice, that he remarked to Mr. Palethorpe they had got hold of a spanker; to which the curate, not knowing in the least whether the observation applied to the horse or the driver, and preoccupied also with his own misadventures, replied it was very possible, as he understood most cabmen were.

Arrived at his apartments, Frank made his wishes known as to the providing a bed for his friend. His landlady appeared somewhat aggrieved at such a proposal at that hour of the night; but surmising from the Reverend Ernest's attire the profession to which he most likely belonged, her respect for the Establishment appeared to overcome her objections, and she promised to do the best in her power. But as another bedroom was out of the question, would the gentleman be content, she asked, with the sofa, if she made it comfortable for him? To this the gentleman demurred a little, as he had never slept on a sofa in his life, he said; but to make everything agreeable, he suggested that if Frank would sleep on the sofa, he had no doubt that he himself could manage with Frank's bed. There was a merry twinkle in Frank Ossett's honest grey eyes as he said he was afraid he should roll off, and elected to remain in his own room.

"And now, old fellow," Frank said, his hearty nature subduing for a time at least his aversion to the curate," we'll have some supper. Mrs. Ellis will manage a pillow and a coverlet, and in the morning we'll see what's to be done."

The Reverend Ernest protested he was no supper eater; nevertheless, when the pleasant little dainties from Frank's larder were produced, he acquitted himself very manfully, and became quite conversational.

"And if it's not impertinent," Frank asked, "what has brought you to London?"

Then the Reverend Ernest Palethorpe drawing his chair towards the fireplace, and nursing his knee with his head inclined to one side, explained how he had come to the Euston Square Station that afternoon for a week's stay in London, that he might attend some of the May meetings; perhaps visit the Royal Academy Exhibition, see the Tower, and, if possible, go down one day to Windsor. To-morrow, he proposed going to a meeting at Exeter Hall.

"Oh !" Frank rejoined, "what's going on there, then ? Niggers ?"

"Niggers, indeed !" the other said. "No; it's a meeting of the Ladies' Benevolent Visiting and Tract Distribution Society, established with a view to the Regeneration of the Struggling Poor, in connection with the Woman's Rights and Female Emancipation Society, when several gifted sisters will address the meeting."

After a pause, the curate said—"Would Mr. Ossett like to accompany him ?"

The twinkle came back to Frank's eyes, as he said nothing would have given him greater pleasure, but most unfortunately he had to attend a consultation at counsel's chambers touching a disputed right of way.

That was a pity, Ernest said, especially as some friends of his—lady friends—who knew Frank, would probably be present.

Associated as Mr. Palethorpe was with Dalesford, Frank's thoughts flew homewards, and thinking of one fair face, he would have given so much to see again, and yet feeling how vain was that hope, he asked eagerly who they were.

"A most worthy Christian lady," the curate answered, simpering, and nursing his leg, "and her daughter, a charming ge-irl ! Mrs. and Miss Dingwall."

" O Lord !" Frank cried. " I mean to say, are they really ?"

" You met them at Brighton, I think ?" the curate continued. " Charming persons, are they not ? It is so refreshing to see such family affection."

" Oh, very !" Frank answered.

" Her mother tells me," the Reverend Ernest continued, " how devoted a daughter Martha is—a gleam of sunshine in the home, and so purely artless and—and—spontaneous !"

I think Mr. Frank had his own views on this point, for he was silent a few seconds, and then said—

" Ah, yes ; it's very touching."

" Very much so," Ernest said. " I think I'll take my boots off. Have you a pair of slippers ?"

" You can have mine," the young fellow said, " they're in that corner, I think," he continued, ringing the bell. " We wont keep the old lady up ; I'll ask her to bring up the kettle and we can turn in when we like."

So saying, he produced his spirit decanters, and invited his guest to mix for himself. The Reverend Ernest assured Frank he was not in the habit of taking anything of a spirituous nature, but he was afraid his supper wouldn't agree with him, as he had a delicate stomach, and perhaps a small quantity of brandy—he preferred the pale if Frank had it—might rectify any existing acidity. Frank sat silently watching him as he stirred and sipped and sniffed, and he longed to ask some questions about Matthew Worsdale's broken-up home, and yet could not bear that he should hear the one name that was so dear to his simple heart uttered by the curate's lips. Then he thought of that gentle face and those soft brown eyes, and looking at his visitor, as he sat with a self-complacent smirk, swinging his foot and sipping his brandy and water, he remembered the rumours he had heard of the hopes that the sickly-looking young curate had dared to entertain of such a prize, till he felt a strange sensation of irritability creeping over him, and he was conscious of a terrible temptation to fall upon and demolish the peaceful Ernest. So, with a great effort, he said suddenly—

"Well, there you are; help yourself and make yourself as comfortable as you can. I am going to bed. Good night." And he lit a candle, and opening the door of communication between the sitting-room and bedchamber, retired.

But he could not sleep. His meeting with the curate had roused many unquiet feelings that would not be laid to rest. Besides, the Reverend Ernest had a way of humming aloud and coughing, and tapping the fender with his foot, which occasionally resulted in a violent displacement of the fire-irons, and this after a while became irritating to a great degree. After a time there was a brief silence, and a stealthy movement in the next room, followed by the tinkling of a spoon against a glass, that suggested the visitor had borne in mind his host's invitation to make himself comfortable, and was acting upon it. Then there was silence again, and Frank was pleasantly dropping into a soft slumber, when he was startled by a loud thud.

"By Jove!" he said, "he's off. I thought he would be!" He could hear the Reverend Ernest saying—

"Tut, tut, tut! How very painful to be sure! I think he might have let me have his bed!"

And then he remembered nothing more till he woke the next morning.

When partly dressed, he opened the door softly, and peeped into the sitting-room. The curate was sleeping the sound sleep which a free conscience, or a guileless heart, is popularly supposed to vouchsafe to its happy possessor. But glancing at the spirit decanter on the table, Frank seemed to take another view of the unconscious curate's slumber, for he said to himself, quietly, and rather irreverently—

"Poor devil! he'd better sleep it off. He's good for another hour, at least!"

So having drest himself, he wrote on a card, which he placed on the table where his guest might see it: " Gone out for an hour. Breakfast at nine. Wash and shave in next room. F. O."

A brisk walk round Kensington Gardens, and across Hyde Park, brought him home again, a few minutes past the hour. On his return, he found the Reverend Ernest had left his couch; for in truth, the landlady, whose respect for his cloth had somewhat abated in proportion to the amount of unexpected trouble he had caused, had not hesitated to go into the sitting-room, during Frank's absence, and having opened the windows, had shaken the curate violently, telling him plainly it was time to get up, as Mr. Ossett always took breakfast punctually at nine.

Frank found his guest endeavouring to shave himself with a rather unsteady hand, and removing, involuntarily, whatever irregularities existed on the surface of the clerical skin; and he answered the young fellow's hearty greeting by saying that he felt very unwell indeed, and had a beastly headache.

Frank, saying cheerily, " Oh, you'll be all right, man, when you have had your breakfast," left him to himself, while he opened and read his own letters that had come by the morning post; and he had just skimmed the contents of the day's paper, when the Reverend Ernest entered the room.

"Well," that gentleman said, "I hope I shall never have to sleep on a sofa again. I declare I feel quite upset."

"Well, old fellow," Frank kindly said, "I am sorry I couldn't give you better accommodation. It was the best I had."

"Oh, yes," the curate said, "I am very much obliged to you, of course, but never again any sofas for me."

"Take an egg or a chop?" Frank said, reddening a little, and drawing his chair to the breakfast table.

"Well, I don't know," the Reverend Ernest answered. "I am afraid my stomach wont bear it."

"Oh, bother your stomach!" Mr. Ossett said. "What's the matter with it?"

"Well," Mr. Palethorpe said, seriously, "you can bother my stomach if you like, but I really thought I should have died in the night. I was that ill—well!" and whatever the degree of health might be that was intended to be indicated by that mode of expression, it was one which evidently defied a fuller description.

However, as was the case with the previous evening's supper, the curate got on with his breakfast much better than might have been expected, from the doubt he appeared to entertain of his own capacity.

"Now, your reverence," Frank said, in his own pleasant way, after they had been eating some time in silence, "what's your programme for the day? I may as well tell you at once, I don't want to be late at the office this morning, for I was dining with Mr. Titheradge last evening, and, perhaps, as a man of business, he'll be all the better pleased if he finds I am punctual to-day."

"Well, really, I don't quite know," Ernest answered; "I must find my lodgings first. Do you think my portmanteau's safe?"

"Ah, I don't know about that," Frank said, with much gravity; "it all depends what's in it. Dreadful place London, sir! There was a young gentleman—a B.A. too, he was—came up only one day last week—he's missing. He was last seen near the Haymarket, at a late hour in the night, and he's never been heard of since."

"Very sad, indeed; very sad!" the Reverend Ernest murmured. "Oh, by-the-way, Mr. Ossett, could you lend me a clean collar?"

"Oh, certainly," Frank said, "anything you want. You may as well have a handkerchief, too, till you find your portmanteau. You wont mind my name in the corner?"

"Oh, not at all," Ernest replied; "I can sew the corner down."

"Eh? Oh, certainly," Frank said. "But you've no money, have you? No, I remember. Shall I let you have a sovereign?"

"You're very good, I am sure, Mr. Ossett," Ernest replied, "but I don't think a sovereign will go very far."

"Eh? Oh, we'll make it two if you like," Frank said. "Stay; you had better have some silver; perhaps you would like to drop the old girl here a shilling or two for her trouble, so here's ten shillings worth and gold."

The Reverend Ernest, saying "Thanks," with the air and in the tone of a man who had just been paid an account that was owing, put the money in his pocket.

"And now," said Frank, "I must be off. I don't suppose I shall see you again, so good-by," and he extended his hand.

"Well," said the curate, "I don't think I need go yet. I should like to write a letter to my auntie in Lincolnshire, if you could oblige me with some paper and envelopes."

"You'll find what you want there," Frank said, somewhat brusquely, as he pushed a small writing-case towards the curate. "Good day."

"Oh!" the Reverend Ernest asked, as Frank

was leaving the room. "Could you let me have a little pomade for my hair?"

"Pomade!" Frank shouted, as he descended the staircase. "No, I never use it! Good-day!"

· "And of all the ungracious, impudent beggars I ever met," he said, as he walked down Seymour Street, "that evangelical prig is the worst! For an innocent young creature, he knows his way about the world as well as any one. Why, I am a baby in his hands! I dare be sworn he wont pay me that two pounds for six years, and then plead the Statute of Limitations. And I am Yorkshire! Oh! my county will blush for me!"

And with a laugh at the remembrance of his night's adventure, he bought a twopenny nosegay of a pretty little street flower-girl, to whom he gave a sixpence and passed on.

Having arrived at the office, he was at once for going to Mr. Titheradge's room to inquire after his kind hostess of the previous evening, when he learnt from a clerk that Mr. Titheradge was engaged with a gentleman, and did not wish to be disturbed. The door of the room was standing ajar, and Frank could not avoid hearing Mr. Titheradge say, in reply probably to a question of the other—

"Stronger, I am glad to say, stronger. Cannot do better than remain another week."

" You are indeed extremely kind, and——" the
other voice was beginning to say, when Frank,
softly approaching, closed the door, and he heard
no more.

Almost immediately afterwards the door was
reopened by Mr. Titheradge, who, without advancing
further, said, " Good morning, Mr. Ossett. Bond
has not returned yet ; would you kindly step round
to Bedford Row with this deed, and say I shall
have the pleasure of calling in the course of an
hour ?"

When Frank returned, the client or visitor had
gone, and Mr. Titheradge was humming a tune in
his peculiar way, as Frank politely inquired after
his own and Mrs. Titheradge's health.

For any change in his manner, Mr. Titheradge
might never have left his office chair and table for
a week. There was not a trace of the genial
hospitable old gentleman of the previous evening,
and Frank had difficulty in identifying the careful,
shrewd man of business before him with the
pleasant, jovial old fellow, who favoured a particular
tavern because the ale was strong, played the
clarionette, cultivated cucumbers and strawberries,
had seen Tom Spring fight a famous battle, yet
almost shed tears at the recollection of his old
pony, and was careful lest Frank should tread
on a toad.

CHAPTER II.

POOR FRANK !

THAT worthy lady, Mrs. Dingwall, and her charming daughter, the artless Martha, had taken apartments at a corner house in Gray's Inn Road, for Martha had argued with much sagacity, that the constant traffic would make it lively. But as it was unfortunately the case that the lively traffic of the day was continued pretty much through the night, and as they had insisted moreover on having a front bed-room, they had not enjoyed that undisturbed night's rest which some lodgers seem to think ought to be guaranteed with the let of the rooms. The result was that their breakfast was not by any means a cheerful meal; Martha appearing bilious and heavy, while her mother was tortured by an irritating suspicion that spiders were crawling on her. Mrs. Dingwall was disposed, too, to consider the metropolis as an evergrown and dirty place, and more than once defiantly stated that if this was Martha's beautiful, grand London, for her part give her Congleton !

To which the "spontaneous" Martha would reply—
"Lor, mar, how you do go on! You're enough to
worrit anybody to death!"

It therefore cost both ladies a slight effort to
appear cheerful and amiable, when they heard the
neat little knock at the street door, which as they
rightly surmised announced the arrival of the
Reverend Ernest Palethorpe. He wore his sickly
smile as usual, and also Frank Ossett's clean collar,
which, with his own guileless manner, made him
as presentable a young person as could be found
that bright May morning in the great world of
London.

The artless Martha sat with her mamma's hand
between her own, measuring with child-like simplicity their respective fingers, or unconsciously picking at the maternal knuckles; while the Reverend
Ernest, smiling sweetly on such mutual affection,
told them in his own complacent way his adventures
on the previous evening,—or—or some of them.

Martha had never—no, never, in the whole
course of her life, heard of anything so truly extra-
ordinary as the meeting of himself and Mr. Ossett!
But was it *really* Mr. Ossett? Yes; but was it
the Mr. Ossett they knew? Well, to be sure! If
she had read it in a book she wouldn't have
believed it! And when the Reverend Ernest,
elated a little perhaps by the success of his narra-

tive, told them how pleased Frank had been to see
him, and how he had hoped that he, the Reverend
Ernest, would call again, with other little fanciful
additions to the facts of the case, not altogether
unusual, I think, with persons who enjoy a
natural buoyancy of spirits and childish simplicity
of heart—the gratified surprise of mother and
daughter was truly refreshing to see.

However, as the meeting in Exeter Hall was
fixed for one o'clock, there was no time to lose.
When the ladies had withdrawn to attire themselves, the gentle curate took from his pocket a
small housewife or needlecase, and with the aid of
a thimble and a needle and thread which it contained, he turned down the corner of Frank's
pocket-handkerchief, and effectually concealed,
though temporarily, the somewhat conspicuous F. O.
that indicated the rightful ownership of the property.

Having elected to walk to the Strand, in compliance with the suggestion of the Reverend Palethorpe, on the grounds, as he stated, that omni-
buses never took you where you wished to go, and
that cabmen were, as a class, abusive persons, who
were only removed by a narrow line from habitual
criminals of the worst class, they started, in accordance with the landlady's directions, by the nearest
way.

But as they became dreadfully bewildered before reaching Holborn, and completely lost themselves in the neighbourhood of Drury Lane, they did not arrive at the Hall until half an hour after the proceedings had commenced, and were in consequence compelled to put up with very inconvenient places.

But once there, as they afterwards admitted, they were amply repaid for their fatigue and trouble. Indeed it was impossible, as the Reverend Ernest sweetly remarked, to be present at such a meeting without hearing soul-stirring words and messages of peace to the bruised heart. Dr. Rachel Gambado, of Bunkumville (Mass.), was in great force; as were also Mrs. Flannel Fowler, and Miss Whyte Grannitt; though the success of the meeting was considered to have been achieved by Mr. Pompey Wampum (New York). His touching reminiscences of slave life in the South, and his eloquent outburst on Liberty—which had nothing whatever to do with the questions before the meeting—were equal to anything the Reverend Ernest had ever heard, and far exceeded the artless Martha's warmest anticipations.

I don't know what became of them after the meeting—they were lost in the crowd of admirers who had met to welcome these advanced spirits of the age; but I believe they adjourned to a con-

fectioner's in the Strand, where Martha ate ices
till her teeth ached—as she said to her mamma, "fit
to drop out;" while her more prudent companions
took cherry brandy and sweet cakes.

However, when Mr. Frank Ossett, having dined
in town, strolled leisurely homewards for the purpose of changing his dress before going to some
place of amusement in the evening, he was surprised by the servant, who opened the door to him,
saying—

"If you please, sir, the gentleman's upstairs,
and has been waiting for you."

"Gentleman?" Frank repeated. "What gentleman?"

"Him as was here last night, sir," the girl said,
"and slep' on the sofy."

"The devil he is!" Frank cried. "Why, what
the deuce does he want?"

"Don't know, sir, I'm sure," the little servant
said; "but he's got his portmantel with him."

As she said these words, Frank turned to her
with a look of such utter dismay in his face,
that she evidently felt it compulsory on her to
add—

"An' he's been here more nor an hour."

I think, as Frank stood blankly staring at the
little servant, and she stood as blankly staring at
him, he was, in a confused way, turning over in his

mind whether he should give the Reverend Ernest
in charge for being found on his premises for an
unlawful purpose, or immediately run down to
Brighton for a few days, leaving things to take
their own course, or at once go upstairs and
demand an explanation, previous to throwing the
curate over the banisters.

So, quite undecided how to act, and scarcely
knowing what he said, he merely replied—

"Quite so. It isn't your fault, of course, Mary.
I'll see to it." And went up stairs deliberately,
and treading heavily, as men sometimes do in a
moment of indecision and annoyance.

The Reverend Ernest Palethorpe was lying on the
sofa, with one of his dusty boots resting on a pillow.

"Well, really!" he said in an almost reproachful tone as Frank entered; "I thought
you were never coming."

"Coming!" Frank repeated, quite at a loss for
a suitable rejoinder. "Coming! By Jove you've
come!"

"Yes," said Ernest, "and I'm dreadfully tired.
What a day I have had! I am nearly walked off
my legs, I declare."

The very simplicity of the young curate's
character, which to Frank's prejudiced view seemed
so like sheer impudence, was too much for the
young fellow; and after an astonished stare of a

few seconds, he could find no better form of expression than by saying—

"I say, Palethorpe ; here, you know—what's your game ?"

"Well," the Reverend Ernest said, cheerfully, "if I could just have a cup of tea I could tell you all I have been doing."

"I don't want to know what you've been doing," Frank said, shortly. "Here, what's that thing ?" And he poked Mr. Palethorpe's portmanteau with his stick.

"That's my portmanteau, if you please," the Reverend Ernest replied, in an injured tone.

"Well, if it is, what's it doing here ?" Frank asked.

"Oh," the Reverend Ernest said, in explanation, "I am not going back to that place in the Hampstead Road. What do you think ? they actually wanted to charge me for a week before I'd ever slept in the house. I never heard of such a thing !"

"You'd taken the rooms, hadn't you ?" Frank asked as brusquely as before.

"Well, I am not going to be imposed upon that way, so I came away," Ernest said.

"Came away ? Do you mean without paying them ?" Frank asked, becoming interested in spite of himself. "How did you do it ?"

" Well," the Reverend Ernest replied, " it seems the woman of the house is subject to fits, and so I just walked out with my portmanteau, and called a cab."

The unwonted spark of anger that had been glistening in Frank's eyes seemed to die out, or to give way to the twinkle that was more in harmony with his good-natured face; and he said in a tone of wonder and with an amazed expression—

" Well, you are a cool beggar! Of all the cool beggars I ever met, if you're not the coolest I'll be hanged ! What are you going to do now ?"

" Why," the curate answered, without the slightest hesitation or embarrassment, " I thought your landlady might find me a bed, or I might sleep on the sofa again."

" No !" Frank said, stoutly and decisively, but with his good-humour perfectly restored. " I don't stand that, Palethorpe. You can get plenty of beds in London without inconveniencing me, or imposing on the people here. If you want some tea"—and he rang the bell—" you shall have it, but after that you must go."

" Then I think it very unkind of you, Mr. Ossett," Ernest answered, rolling his head from side to side on the sofa pillow, and pouting; " and I didn't expect this treatment from an old friend."

" But I am not an old friend," Frank said.

" I scarcely ever spoke to you till I saw you last night. Oh," he said, as the servant appeared at the door, " bring the tea as soon as you can, Mary, will you ?"

" Oh, never mind your tea, thank you," Ernest said, pouting as before. " I can do without it, I dare say."

" Bring the tea, Mary," Frank said, relenting a little, as the girl left the room. " You must see, my good fellow, how unreasonable——"

" I'll thank you, Mr. Ossett," the curate replied, still lying on the sofa, " not to address me as your good fellow."

" Well, then," said Frank, smiling in spite of himself: " Reverend Sir—will that do ?—how unreasonable you are. I can't offer you a bed, and I wont let you sleep upon the sofa, and there's an end of the matter. But I am going to have some tea, and if you like you shall have some too; but do as you please."

And with that he went into his own room, and commenced to change his dress.

Whether the short time that intervened before Frank's reappearance, or the preparations for the tea, had smoothed the ruffled surface of the curate's temper, he had certainly so far recovered his accustomed serenity, that when he saw Frank in his evening dress he said—

" Bless us, how smart you are! Are you going to a party?"

" Mary," Frank said to the girl, who was still in the room preparing the table, " don't be out of the way. I shall want you shortly to fetch a cab for Mr. Palethorpe. Now then," he continued, addressing the reverend gentleman, " have some tea: help yourself."

" Well," Ernest said, drawing up a chair to the table, " I've a dreadful headache again. I think I should have liked some coffee instead—it isn't well to drink too much tea. Oh!" he suddenly said, " who do you think I saw to-day, of all others? I am sure it was he, though very much altered."

" Oh, I don't know," Frank said, with indifference ; " old Mother What-d'ye-call-'em ?—Dingwall ?"

" I don't think it at all becoming in you, Mr. Ossett," the Reverend Ernest said, in his reproachful tones, " to speak in that way of a worthy person like Mrs. Dingwall."

" Oh, yes, I know," Frank replied, impatiently ; " get on : who was it?"

" Why," said Ernest, soaking a biscuit in his tea, and nibbling it with much gusto, " that dreadful man who set fire to Worsdale's mill."

" What did you say?" Frank asked, looking scared, and setting down his cup.

" That foreman—you must remember him—I really forget the creature's name," Ernest said.

" You don't mean Boothroyd ?" Frank asked, turning very white and then flushing crimson.

" Yes, I do," Ernest said ; " that man—the one who thought proper to make love to Miss Dolly."

As the possible truth of what the curate said, and the entirely new view of the matter which his words created, rushed through the poor young fellow's mind, his face altered so perceptibly, and he seemed for a few seconds so utterly prostrated and wretched, that even the Reverend Ernest, pushing his cup to the tea-tray to be replenished, observed it and said—

" What's the matter ? Are you ill ? Better have some brandy."

" No," Frank said, with an effort at self-control ; " it's nothing—I shall be better presently— wait a moment; yes, I'll have a spoonful of brandy— and you too," he said taking the liquor from the side-board with an unsteady hand. " Help yourself; and for God's sake, Mr. Palethorpe, tell me all you know !"

·I think we have seen enough of the Reverend Ernest Palethorpe to know that, when he could oblige a friend with a narrative of the wickedness, real or supposed, of another party, he would not be reluctant to furnish it; and so, having refreshed

himself as invited, he gave Frank a very minute
and animated account of the interview between
Mr. Worsdale and Joe Boothroyd, which terminated
in Joe's ignominious dismissal, as he described it,
and which was followed by the calamity of the
conflagration at the mill.   Frank listened with intense anxiety, and when the Reverend Ernest
paused for further refreshment, said hoarsely—

"Go on, please."

But when, having referred to the fire, he mentioned the suspicion that was attached to Joe Boothroyd in connexion with it, Frank said quietly—

"I don't believe it.   He had no motive."

Though, from my own more intimate knowledge
of the worthy young minister's character, I am disposed to think he would willingly have spared
Frank (and himself) a description of the lovers'
interview beneath the old sycamore tree on Daisy
Hill, yet being driven, by Frank's assertion of an
absence of motive, to make his own views on the
matter consistent and sound, he was led into telling, little and little, the whole of the story
even as he admitted he had overheard it, to the
avowal of love by Joe, and the emotion of
Dolly.

"And they never knew you were listening, or
were even near them?" Frank asked.

"No; I should think not, indeed!" Ernest

answered, pleasantly, " for I lay as still as a little mouse."

" Oh, you did, did you ?" Frank said again.

" Yes, and I heard every word that passed," the Reverend Ernest said, with a self-complacent smirk. And then he told Frank how he had picked up the bunch of little faded flowers that Dolly had thrown away, and how he had sent them to her anonymously, to all of which Frank listened quietly, but breathing rather shortly, and with an unusual bright look in his dark grey eyes, till the Reverend Ernest Palethorpe, warming with his subject—as such persons do when self is the subject on which they are dilating—described the interview between himself and Mr. Worsdale, and how, thanks to his friendly instrumentality, Joe Boothroyd's discomfiture and disgrace were completed, when, to the reverend gentleman's amazement, Frank started to his feet, and striking the table with his clenched fist, cried—

" Then confound you for an infernal sneak ! It's the most blackguard thing I ever heard ! Get out of my room, and take your d——d portmanteau with you, or I'll throw you both out of the window !"

And turning up the sleeves of his coat, his eyes glaring with passion, he really seemed about to carry out his threat on the instant.

The Reverend Ernest Palethorpe, who had never regarded his conduct in that affair in any but the most favourable light, and who, to the last day of our acquaintance, seemed never to have a suspicion he had adopted any but a strictly prudent, proper, and friendly course, sat for a few seconds in speechless amazement at this hostile demonstration, and then said, with perfect simplicity—

"Good gracious, Mr. Ossett, what have I done?"

"What have you done!" Frank thundered out. "What right had you to step between them? Who are you to dare to eaves-drop and spy, that you might work your miserable spite on the girl who rejected you? Don't interrupt me in my own room, sir!—I say, rejected you! I know she did scorn and despise you, as any one with a true woman's heart, or man's either, must do! What have you done? I'll tell you what you have done. You have made two better people than ever you were, you canting humbug, miserable for life; you have set a father against his own child, a dear, good girl" (and here his voice broke a little) "if there ever was one! It was through your petty envy and cursed slander that Boothroyd was discharged; by that he may have been driven to desperation, and perhaps revenge; and if he did commit the crime you say, why you have driven him to it! And Matthew Worsdale may date his ruin from the malicious intermeddling of a man who pretends to be a Christian and a minister! There's the door—get out! Confound you, get out! Mary, call a cab—anything! I wont have you here!"

And with that he rung the bell violently.

I don't know whether during this violence of Frank's it occurred to the Reverend Ernest that his conduct in the affair might be just susceptible of another colour than that in which he himself had viewed it, and that it required some defence from him, or whether he felt some righteous indignation that his disinterested actions should be so maligned, for he answered with a little warmth, and not quite prudently—

" Well, Mr. Ossett, I really don't know what you mean. That Boothroyd-man was a presumptuous person; and Miss Dolly Worsdale is nothing better than a flirting young jade!"

I believe Frank made no reply to this, but he opened the door of the room; and as the servant girl, aroused by the violent ringing of the bell, was hastening upstairs, she was met by a portmanteau coming rapidly down; and from the unusually hasty way in which that article of luggage was followed by the Reverend Ernest, as well as from the fact that during the remainder of his stay in town he complained of an attack of lumbago, which necessitated some deliberation on his part when taking a chair, I have been given to understand there were reasons for so precipitate a departure.

Of course, I don't defend Mr. Frank Ossett's violence of speech and manner; and it is only fair to that honest but impulsive young fellow to say at once how much he regretted it. I know this sudden ebullition of passion towards his guest— self-invited though that guest was, and a minister of the Church—is not to be defended or excused on any grounds; and had Frank been an older or more worldly-minded person, he would perhaps have heard all the curate had to say, and if his own opinion had been adverse, reserved it; but, poor lad, he was not a model young man—as the Reverend Ernest was; he was simply a kindhearted, generous fellow, loyal to his friend, faithful to his love (the love he had never dared to tell but still cherished), an easy prey to men more designing than himself, anything but brilliant or clever, impetuous and perhaps not always just; but still, underlying all his many foibles and vanities and fopperies, there was a stout love for truth, an utter scorn for shams of all kinds and by what names soever dignified, a thorough detestation of meanness in any form, and a manly courage to own himself wrong when convicted of a fault.

4—2

So, though in after years he often laughed at this adventure, when some of us (who were privileged to do so) ventured to remind him of it, he always spoke with strong self-depreciation while advancing the plea of intense annoyance and provocation.

Left to himself in his own room, the poor lad sat down to reflect on what he had heard. I do not think he had for a moment any bitter feeling towards Joe Boothroyd. He was conscious his rival had some advantage over himself, and he accepted his defeat as a brave young fellow should. He had hoped he might one day win the heart of the one girl he had seen to love, and from hoping had begun to fancy that the two young hearts must come together at last, and beat side by side to the end, and then perhaps, in a better and purer life, be still united far from all the cares and envies of this world. And now he was awakened from the happy vision, and lo! it was only a dream after all!

He sat down in his little room and cried, with the passionate grief of his boyhood when some cherished fancy had been roughly checked, and he felt the bitter pangs of a first disappointment. But to honest grief and not unworthy anger he gave way thus; and the simple manliness of his character was never better indicated than when with unabated love for Dolly, and involuntary respect, wholly unalloyed by envy or malice for her lover, and knowing the race he had honestly hoped to win was hopelessly lost, he sat down and cried, like the foolish, honest lad poor Frank undoubtedly was.

CHAPTER III.

AT HOME IN PEDLINGTON.

T has been said of the handsome and wealthy city of Manchester, that for two hundred days out of the three hundred and sixty-five you may expect rain; but whether this is a general impression, founded on experience, or owes its rise merely to the lively fancy or sarcastic humour of the person who made that remark to me, I never remained sufficiently long in that huge place to decide. Perhaps the natural humidity of the climate (assuming the statement to be true) may have conveyed a lesson to the population, moral and salutary; for certainly if there is one place more than another where the inhabitants appear to be always providing against "a rainy day," where business seems to be their pleasure, while their very pleasures have an air of business, it is surely this north-western English capital, with its palatial warehouses, vast factories, and forest of tall chimneys. But the most loyal citizen or enthusiastic admirer will scarcely venture

to claim for it a position as a fashionable resort.
Of course fashion is there, as where is it not now-
a-days? but it goes there to the people, and the
people go elsewhere for it. Comfort, wealth,
luxury, intelligence (of the highest), enterprise,
and progress—everything that is born of commercial success or conduces to it—may be met
with in one form or another on all sides; but as
a resort for people of pleasure and fashion, we
should scarcely select the gigantic Lancashire hive,
in which the queen-bee is Commerce, and where
the drones are crowded out by the workers in their
incessant efforts to meet Demand with Supply.

Especially, too, in the middle of May, when
London is rapidly filling and drawing thousands
for the annual sojourn of the season, it may
appear somewhat strange that such a mere man of
pleasure as Major Maismore was, and whom we at
once recognise by the familiar white hair and dark
moustache, should be passing through St. Ann's
Square in the afternoon, in fact on the very hour
of the very day that Mr. Pompey Wampum (N. Y.)
was addressing in Exeter Hall a large assembly,
whom he called " brudders in the Lor'."

But votaries of pleasure, as they are called, are
also frequently birds of passage—and some, I believe, are even birds of prey—and they wing their
eccentric flights wherever their fancy listeth, or

where instinct suggests an early worm or a recent crumb.

I should be reluctant to class the Major with cither of these divisions, nor do I recollect having recorded any instance whereby the acute reader can lay his hand on the Major's shoulder, and say with authority, "Thou art the man;" but having referred to the fowls of the air for an illustration, I may go a little further, and consider him a natural affinity of that bird, which is neither migratory nor carnivorous, but whose sagacity is second to none; and one, moreover, that, I am told, is not uncommon in society, nor altogether unknown in the highest circles, and is called a Rook.

If, as has been observed by more than one philosopher, we, who are lords of the creation, may with advantage consider the characters of certain of the lower animals for the improvement of our own—as we (like the sluggard) may go to the ant to learn wisdom, to the dog for courage and fidelity, for patience and endurance to the horse, or meekness under insult, and a primitive simplicity in choice of food to the amiable donkey—so we may certainly pick up a little astuteness and worldly knowledge from a careful observation of our feathered exemplar in black. Please to remember he has not the vulgar and carnal appetites of his first cousin,

the Crow, nor the absurd self-assertiveness and incessant chattering of his more remote connexion,
the Daw, with the affectation of dwelling in church
towers and old castles—(I believe we all know members of the large Daw family, who aspire to live in a
cathedral close, or under the shadow of a noble old
house)—nor does he emulate the eccentricities and
that dangerous talent for imitation possessed by his
big relative the Raven (qualities that sometimes
cause that otherwise sapient bird to be taken young
and retained in honourable captivity, that he may
divert his captors by crying " Ostler," or " Cook");
but with some of the characteristics of each, our
very sagacious friend the Rook steers clear of the
faults of all. He prefers wholesome grain and
fresh food to carrion; but, mind you, he will
accept carrion if the alternative is starvation, and
which, I take it, is a true Epicurean philosophy.
He leaves the miserable noise and tittle-tattle of
town life to that inveterate gossip the Daw, and
fixes his residence in some remote group of trees,
where he can caw his sentiments to his sable
brotherhood without let or hindrance ; or in some
recognised rookery, the respectability of which is
beyond question, and where he is not considered
as a tenant-at-will, but rather as a permanent occu-
pier on a repairing lease, where every March he
puts his house in order preparatory to the advent

of his annual brood. And this sagacious bird, against whom we cannot charge the Raven's voracity or open theft, may, in the doctrine of metempsychosis, represent the Major, who, with his habitual quiet and watchful manner, taking in all details in a comprehensive glance, while apparently looking simply before him, paused for a few seconds on the footway, to allow two ladies to pass before him from the door of a shop to the brougham waiting their convenience near the pavement.

The amiable and philanthropic Lady Petitoe and her attached friend and companion Miss Skimple, had been making a few purchases at a draper's, and Miss Skimple was handing a small leaflet to a woman who was asking charity, when raising her eyes she met the steady gaze of the Major. Our dear Skimple started and changed colour, as she had done a twelvemonth before when she had met Mr. Edward Sherwin at Worsdale House, or Captain Clarence at Redwell, and for a moment she, usually so self-possessed, appeared distressed and embarrassed. This might arise from a doubt in her mind, whether having relinquished all connexion with Matthew Worsdale and his family, the estrangement ought not to be extended to his acquaintances as well; or it might be that some sudden and transitory emotion ruffled the calm surface of the Skimple nature; but whatever it was, she turned cold, and made a sort of half bow. The Major in his turn looked at her with an expression of mild astonishment, and politely raised his hat in acknowledgment of her recognition, slight as it was.

Lady Petitoe having directed the coachman to drive home, turned to her companion, who was fanning herself with her handkerchief, and leaning back in the corner of the carriage—

"Ah! it's hot, dear, ain't it?" Lady Petitoe observed.

Miss Skimple said, "Yes, it was, very." And then said, as if to herself though aloud, "How strange, to be sure!"

"What, dear?" the other asked.

But Miss Skimple only said, "Nothing." And the drive home was passed in silence on her part, except such replies, brief and cautious, as Lady Petitoe's steady current of talk required.

The Major was not addicted to soliloquy—(excuse me for reminding you, that while Daws and Ravens learn to speak easily, no one has ever taught a Rook to talk)—but he said, half aloud—

"Devilish odd, to be sure!"

He had walked on a few yards, very much preoccupied by his own thoughts, when he became conscious of an uncomfortable feeling of irritation creeping over him, and he found it was caused by a small boy who had been dodging about his footsteps, now in front, looking back into his face, and getting almost under his very feet, then on one side and then on the other, until at last he said—

" Confound you! get away you little beggar!" and prepared to give the lad a swish with the light walking cane he carried, when the boy disappeared from his side and seemed to pop up again in front of him, with his legs set wide apart and his hands thrust into his trousers pockets, which seemed to reach to the knees.

" Hollo!" said the lad, " I say, don't you re-member? How d'ye do, Mr. Sherwin?"

The Major did not recognize poor little Phil in his altered dress and circumstances, for he said, stroking his dark moustache—his habit when in doubt or earnest thought—

" Eh? Why, who the deuce——?"

" Why," Phil said, grinning, " you remember Mr. Worsdale—before the fire? I'm Phil. Are you going to see father, sir? He'll be in for tea at five."

For some moments the Major remained silent, stroking his moustache and looking quietly at Phil; then he said, " How are you, my little man? Come along with me, little Worsdale."

And so he led the way to a confectioner's shop,

only a few yards distant. When seated at a little table in the dinner room, the Major said—

" Now, my man, give your orders ; what will you take ?"

" Nothing, thank you, sir," Phil answered, " unless you do."

" Well," the Major said, smiling, and with an amused look in his eyes, " since you have been so pressing, I shall go in for jelly, I think."

The attendant placed some sweets on the table, but for some reason of his own, Phil would not taste them until the Major had commenced, and then he fell to with a boy's own enjoyment.

" Were you going to see father, sir," Phil asked, " when I saw you ?"

" Not exactly," the Major answered. " You see, my little friend, I don't know his address."

Phil soon removed that difficulty, and eating and talking, told the Major he must be sure to call between one and two or five and six, as at other times his father might be out.

" Ah," the Major said, " those are the very hours most inconvenient to myself ; but I will see what I can do."

He had not much difficulty in learning from Phil such particulars as he cared to know in connexion with Matthew's change of circumstances. The little fellow had told him very fairly of their present position in the world, and how much his father had taken to heart his sadly altered fortunes. Also how Miss Skimple, with characteristic fore-sight, had relieved Mr. Worsdale of the unpleasant task of proposing a termination of her services by suggesting it herself, and how she had left them somewhat suddenly, or, in the boy's own phrase, had " hooked it precious quick," and was now, Phil believed, living somewhere in Manchester, as he had seen her one day and said, " How d'ye do, ma'am ? But I don't think she heard me," he continued, simply, " for she looked another way." Prissy was still at home, he said, keeping father's house, and Tim ? Yes, Tim was all right and getting along somehow.

" And the other one—your other sister, where is she ?" the Major asked, looking on the floor, and drawing figures with the end of his cane.

The boy making no reply, the Major repeated the question, and looking up saw poor Phil's lips quivering, and two large tears, which he was endeavouring to repress by a violent gulp of the tart he was eating, ready to roll down his round face.

" Good God !" cried the Major, " what's the matter, my man ? She is not—not——" and he didn't finish the sentence.

" N-n—no, sir," the little fellow said, as he

tried to check with a pink cotton handkerchief the tears that were falling on his corduroys. "No, sir; I know what you mean—at least we don't think so; but she's gone."

"Gone!" the Major said. "What on earth do you mean?"

"Please, sir, I can't say any more," Phil faltered out, "I must go now—and—and thank you."

The poor lad was in such evident distress, and was making such efforts to control it, that the Major had not the heart to question him further, but having taken down Matthew Worsdale's address, he shook hands kindly with Phil, slipping a crown piece into his hand as he did so. This, Phil was going to decline, but the Major said in the pleasant way which, if not natural to him, he knew so well how to assume, "No, no, you must take care of it for me till I see you again. I always spend loose silver—when I have it, especially in a confectioner's shop; never could take care of my money in my life—never."

Phil thought for a moment or two, and then saying, "All right, sir, thank you!" turned out of the shop and ran up the street.

The Major stood at the shop door, looking after him. Then he stroked his dark moustache, and saying, "Poor little chap!" turned thoughtfully away.

When Matthew returned home that evening, he found Phil already there, and but that Matthew himself was rather late, he would have also found Prissy standing with an empty teakettle in her hand, and listening with heightening colour and sparkling eyes to her brother's account of his interview with the man whom she had known as Captain Clarence when at Redwell, and as Mr. Edward Sherwin at Dalesford.

As it was, Matthew found her on her knees before the kitchen fire, with a pair of Tim's big gloves that he had given her to mend on her little hands, poking small pieces of newspaper between the bars of the grate, in vain efforts to light the fire and boil the water. Phil was on the other side of her, endeavouring to fan the light into a steady flame by the aid of his cap.

Matthew sat sullenly down, and said, shortly—

"This ought to have been done before."

It was scarcely more than two months since Dolly had left home, but the time, short as it was, seemed to have greatly told upon him. The lines in the face were deeper, and there was a perceptible hollow under the eyes, and in the formerly firm and square cheeks; his hair too was longer, and more shaggy and white. The habit he had acquired, after the reverse in his affairs, of carrying his head forward, with the eyes cast down, had

become now a confirmed stoop, giving a roundness
to the shoulders, and adding materially to the appearance of age. He had never spoken on the
subject of Dolly's departure, since the night she
went away, and his other children, even Prissy
herself, had grown to fear his presence. The poor
little girl, on whom had suddenly devolved those
cares her sister had discharged so easily and pleasantly, was sadly out of place, and quite over-
weighted by her many little but troublesome responsibilities. A few months ago, she would have
surmounted her difficulties, to some extent at least,
to her father's grim satisfaction, I daresay, and
certainly to her own; but the times were changed
now she felt, and her pretty little coquetting ways,
and fresh young voice, seemed to have lost the
charm they had of old. Whether Matthew had
begun to have some doubts of his elder son, in
connexion with the crime he had attributed to poor
Dolly, or whether it was only another indication of
his grief and general dissatisfaction, he never by
any chance exchanged a word with Mr. Tim. The
youth had, for some time past avoided, as far as
possible, his father's company, but he confessed to
Priscilla, on one occasion, as having been extremely
embarrassed when he had casually met his father
in the street, and Matthew had merely looked
him in the eyes and had passed on.

"Could he have known me, Pris, do you think?" he had asked; "or what is the governor up to?"

"Poor, dear papa!" Prissy had said in reply. "It all comes of poor Dolly going away. I know we shall all go to the workhouse together," and then she had begun to cry, and Mr. Tim taking up his hat, and wildly chirruping with his lips and teeth, would go out for a stroll.

About a month after Dolly's departure, her sister had received a letter from her, with the London post-mark, telling her not to have any fear on her account, as she was quite safe, and was getting well again.

"I have been very ill, my darling," the letter said, "and at one time, I believe, those about me thought I should never be a trouble or a grief to any one again. But I remember nothing of all this myself, it all seemed a long troubled dream, and I am afraid I recollect nothing distinctly after father saw me in his room; nor could I be made to understand that it was not only yesterday that all this happened. Kiss dear father for me, Prissy; be always good and true to him, my dearest; and tell him gently, with my love—more love than ever he can know I feel—that he has misjudged me; but I am sure God will bring us together again, here or in a better world, and then he will know me for his loving child once more."

Poor, little Prissy, who had read and re-read, and kissed and cried over Dolly's simple letter, many times during the day, had ventured in the evening to tell her father, but he had only said, "Oh!" by way of reply, and had remained silent. But as Priscilla, either purposely or by chance, had left the letter on the table when she retired to her room for the night, Matthew finding he was alone, had read it carefully once or twice. Prissy, who, with her accustomed thoughtlessness, had quite forgotten the next day where she had left it, had already begun to lament its loss, and inquire of her two brothers if they had seen it, when her father, taking it from his breast-pocket, said—

"Is that the one, my dear? I found it on the table last night. You should take better care of your letters, or you'll lose them."

Beyond that he made no other remark about it. In the evening, as he was going to bed, he passed the little room where Phil slept, the door of which stood partly open. The lad having been sent on an errand that evening, was later than usual, and was at that moment saying his prayers by his bed-side aloud, as many young folks do. Something the little boy said attracted his father's attention, and, unseen by Phil, he stood and listened. It was probably some little simple and earnest prayer of his own, for it ended by saying—

5—2

"And, pray God, bless dear father, and bring poor Dolly home again. Amen."

Matthew went softly to his room, and began to undress slowly ; but when the house was quite still, and Phil's regular and long-drawn breath denoted his deep and peaceful sleep, the old fellow returned quietly to the boy's bedside, and gently kissing the placid, round face that lay on the pillow, said, softly—

"Amen ! my little lad ! With all my heart, Amen !"

When poor Prissy discovered that all her efforts to boil the water with odd pieces of lighted paper were likely to prove utterly futile, and that her father had more than once indicated by a look, or a short, discontented grunt or cough his own growing impatience, she thought it would be· a good way to divert the gathering storm if Phil were to relate to him his afternoon's interview with Mr. Sherwin. But her tactics were unsuccessful, for Matthew showed no interest in the matter, whatever he might feel, merely saying as usual, "Oh ?"—that unpleasant and formal rejoinder which leaves one no opening for prolonging the conversation. This was very damping to the volatile spirits of Miss Priscilla; for that impulsive young lady, when she had heard Phil's account of the meeting, had fancied that Mr. Sherwin would immediately hasten to relieve her father of all his embarrassments, propose to marry her, induce Dolly to return, and that they would all live happily for evermore.

You see Miss Priscilla had been accustomed for some time to read that pleasant kind of narrative literature into which such delightful, but not strictly probable incidents; are occasionally introduced ; and though Truth is admitted to be stranger than any Fiction, I think its strangeness does not lie quite in that direction. Indeed, in that very common-place work which we may call " Every-day Life," such romantic and agreeable deliverances from trouble either do not occur at all, or at such wide intervals, that perhaps neither you nor I could find the places where they are set down.

Later in the evening that engaging young gentleman, Mr. Tim Worsdale, came in for his tea. The order of the little house, which had suffered a good deal under the presidency of Miss Priscilla, was not improved by the irregular hours and conduct of her elder brother ; partly that he considered his own convenience of the first im-portance, but principally because he wished to avoid, as far as possible, all association with his father, Mr. Tim required his sister to keep his tea and toast hot in the little side oven until it pleased

his excellency to ask for them. The little housekeeper, with more responsibilities already on her
weak hands than she could well discharge, had protested with tears against this arbitrary conduct;
but with her elder brother's ability to say cutting
things to any one who was weaker than himself,
she had gradually yielded to his requirements, and
accepted the additional trouble as part of her lot
in life. Perhaps he was the only member of the
little family on whom the departure of Dolly had
not left some mark of sorrow and regret. He
missed her housewifely skill, and felt, as an essen-
tially selfish nature necessarily would, the difference in the domestic comforts which her absence
caused; but otherwise he felt that absence to be
very likely a relief. He knew that Dolly had
estimated him at his right value long since; and
he had felt besides that latterly she had a power
over him, which, if she had been tempted to
exercise it, would have been unpleasant for himself. But for all that, with little or no grief for
the poor girl's suffering and unmerited disgrace,
he had a feeling of shame for his miserable share
in the matter, which caused him to be very silent
when her name was mentioned, and to slink away
as soon as possible. When Prissy received the
letter referred to, and at the thought of poor
Dolly's danger gave way to a burst of passionate

grief, Mr. Tim, for the first time, seemed to realise the baseness of his own conduct. With her usual impetuosity and romantic exaggeration, Prissy had pictured her sister homeless and wretched, left to die, as she said, " on a door-step, or in a ditch, with no one near her to kiss her poor face, and to love her, who had been so loving to them all." And at such a dismal picture Phil had cried heartily, and blubbered out his intention of there and then setting off to look for her — a proposal that was at once overruled by his more worldly brother, who opportunely reminded him that a stupid young fool like him could do no good. But Mr. Tim was, in his own way, somewhat affected, and his cheerful and engaging manners were considerably clouded. When Dolly's name was mentioned afterwards he would say—" Don't begin on that, Pris. Dolly's all right ;" but he would be distraught, and more churlish than before.

So, when on this night, he took his tea and toast, which he complained were " not warm through," and Prissy and Phil related to him, as they had already done to their father, the incident of the meeting with Mr. Sherwin, and the intention expressed by that gentleman of calling to see them, Mr. Tim rejoined, with a sniggering laugh—

"This is a nice place for a swell to come to, I
don't think ! Be sure you get out the best china
teapot, Pris. Not this black thing with the broken
spout—and all the family plate, at least all that
the fire didn't melt ; and curl your hair, my dear ;
and Doctor" (for so this young wag used to call
Phil since the boy had been in the surgeon's
employment) "you must change your trousers ;
swells like Squire Sherwin or Major-General
Colonel Clarence can't abear the sight of corduroys."

And with such playful speeches and harmless
witticisms he cheered the little home he had helped
to make so desolate.

Whatever Mr. Tim's views might be on the
probability of Mr. Sherwin calling to see them in
their altered circumstances, the next afternoon,
when Matthew Worsdale had gone back to the
factory, and the two boys were at their respective
places of business, Prissy, left alone in the house,
was startled and terribly confused, when answering
a knock at the outer door, she saw Mr. Edward
Sherwin himself.

As she stood for a moment or two, unable in
her embarrassment to speak a word, her visitor
thought he had never seen her look half so lovely
before. It was quite a year since they had met,
and twelve months at that period of life make a

great change sometimes in the appearance of a young girl. Her recent troubles, too, had invested her with a certain womanly air, which in no way lessened her attractiveness. Mr. Sherwin, taking her hand, led her trembling and blushing to a seat, and sat down by her side. His respectful tenderness towards herself, his kind and gentle inquiries for her father in the low voice she remembered so well at Redwell, aroused so many associations, that of course poor Prissy had recourse to her usual relief under circumstances of embarrassment or excitement, and gave way to a flood of tears. She thought many times afterwards how foolish it was, and yet she could not regret the weakness when she remembered how tenderly he had endeavoured to comfort her. When, after a while she was able to control her emotion, she described, frankly and artlessly her father's reverses ; and then Mr. Sherwin, warned by Phil's distress the previous day, ventured cautiously to inquire about Dolly. Poor Prissy gave way again at this, but she explained that her father had had a dreadful quarrel with her sister, and Dolly had in consequence left home. And thus Mr. Sherwin, by dexterously putting his questions, or suggesting reasons, learned little by little as much as she knew of Dolly's attachment, and her father's anger in consequence.

" And this gentleman, who is fortunate enough to have secured your dear sister's love, was he a resident in Dalesford?" Mr. Sherwin had asked.

" He wasn't quite a gentleman," Prissy answered. " At least, I mean to say, not what would be called so, though papa used to like him so much—he was one of his people."

" What do you mean?" Mr. Sherwin asked. " Not one of the mill people, surely?"

" No, not quite that," Prissy said ; " he was the foreman; his name was Boothroyd."

Mr. Sherwin had ventured to retain his hold of the little hand he had taken when he conducted her to the seat, and Prissy had felt comforted by this innocent mark of his friendship and cordiality ; but at the mention of Joe Boothroyd's name, his fingers had clutched her hand so convulsively, that she uttered a suppressed cry of pain and endeavoured to withdraw it.

" I beg your pardon," he said, " I hope I didn't hurt you ? Something startled me at the moment."

" I don't think you saw Mr. Boothroyd when you were at Dalesford ?" Prissy asked.

" No, I think not," Mr. Sherwin answered. Then he asked, after a pause of a few seconds, " Has your father heard from Mr. Boothroyd ?"

" No," the girl answered, " or at least, we have never heard him say so."

" I am sorry to hear this," Mr. Sherwin continued, " though these differences will occur in all families. Your father, my dear Priscilla, a most worthy and estimable man, has yet very strong prejudices, and, I may almost say, obstinacy. You remember his arbitrary condition, that we should not exchange letters or communicate in any way until he had reason to believe our feelings could never change——as if my feelings," he added, pressing the little hand that lay confidingly in his own, " ever could change !"

They sat thus silently for some time, the young girl's face radiant and happy, and Mr. Sherwin looking before him as if at some far distant object, but with a keen and thoughtful expression. Suddenly he said—

" What time does your father return ?"

" At five, generally," Prissy answered. " Do stop and see him, Mr. Sherwin ; it will be such a comfort for him to meet an old friend."

" Unfortunately, I cannot have that pleasure, this evening," Mr. Sherwin said, in a tone of vexation and referring to his watch. " It is now half-past four, and I must leave Manchester at five."

" Leave Manchester !" Prissy exclaimed ; " and not see father !"

" I shall come again, my dear little girl," Mr. Sherwin answered. " You may rely on that."

They stood talking, however, till the clock was on the stroke of five, and then Mr. Sherwin hurried away. Prissy told him, if he turned down the street he would be pretty sure to meet her father on his way home. I suppose he misunderstood her, for he took the other direction.

When Matthew returned home that evening, he found his little daughter unusually excited, and though he was constrained to wait some time before the water in the kettle would so much as simmer on the fire that she had just made, yet she looked so bright and pretty that he forbore to complain, and sat down in silence. Watching for what she thought was a fitting moment to impart her joyful intelligence, she ventured to tell him at last, how Mr. Edward Sherwin had called, and left the house only a short time. Matthew showed more interest than he had manifested for some time ; but it was scarcely as pleasant as Prissy had anticipated, for he said, sharply—

" He ought not to have come without advising me. That was contrary to our understanding ; or at least he ought to have awaited my return."

Prissy endeavoured to make such excuses as she deemed best, such as his engagements elsewhere, as he had told her, ; but her father said—

" Well, well; I don't suppose he'll trouble us again, my dear."

Miss Priscilla's instinct, however, decided otherwise, at least we may infer so; for the next day she busied herself in trimming up the little house, and disposing of the furniture in the front parlour to the best advantage. She also found time during the forenoon to try over one or two of her sparkling little Italian songs, jumping up from her seat now and then to poke 'the kitchen fire, and stir some soup that was simmering in a saucepan on the hob.

And this womanly instinct of her's, as we often find is the case, arrived at a more just conclusion than her father's reason; for about the same hour in the afternoon, when again alone in the house, she was aroused by the same kind of knock, and Mr. Sherwin again presented himself.

His quick glance detected in an instant the change in Prissy's dress, and the improved appearance of the house; and an almost imperceptible smile indicated that he guessed his return had been anticipated.

He explained his presence by saying, that the charming interview of the previous day had caused him to miss the London express train that evening, and he had preferred to defer his departure. Matthew's name having been mentioned, Prissy told him as gently as she could what Matthew had said on the subject of his visit; and Mr. Sherwin looked grave, and stroked his dark moustache.

" Perhaps he is right ; I ought to have seen him first," he said. " Yes; I feel now that would have been the more correct course ; but he cannot know how much I wished to see my dear Priscilla again."

They sat as before—he holding Prissy's hand in his. I do not think it occurred to the girl that she was acting imprudently or thoughtlessly. I know our dear and very estimable friends Miss Skimple and Miss Whyte Grannit would have been above such weakness—even had the occasion been presented ; but the cases are not parallel.

They had a large field for their energy and sympathy among the Struggling Poor, and their own enslaved sisterhood ; whereas our little Priscilla, romantic if you please, but innocent and trusting, impulsive and weak, dearly fond of admiration, and a coquette by nature (as many good women have been when at her age), with no other associates than her soured and grumbling father, and her unsympathetic brothers ; and besides, left for so long a time each day to her own thoughts and fancies, may be excused, I hope, when in the presence of a stronger will than her own, she found herself listening with pride and pleasure to the

whispered words of love and admiration which the
man of the world by her side knew so well how
to utter.

"Still I would not for the world annoy your
excellent father," Mr. Sherwin said, recurring
for a few moments to the previous subject of their
conversation; "and this, my darling, must be our
last interview."

"Our last interview!" Prissy repeated.

"*Here*, I mean," he continued. "Perhaps we
may meet again, some day, at some place, that—
but in the meantime I will write to your good
father—yes; I will write to him."

"Why not see him, Mr. Sherwin?" Prissy
asked.

But taking out his watch and pointing to the
hour—close upon five o'clock, he assured her business of importance called him that very night to
London; and with that he took a hasty and tender
farewell, and Miss Priscilla was left alone to think
over the many tender words he had spoken. An
idea—which his words had in some way suggested,
but certainly not defined—of a clandestine interview, with the pleasant suspense and excitement
inseparable from it, pleased her romantic fancy;
and, I dare say, the trifling deception she would
have to exercise towards her father, and even
brothers, did not render it the less interesting and

acceptable. Perhaps if our little love affairs could be deprived of every element of mystery, and our meetings be arranged without the requirements of ingenuity or secresy, so as to be simply matter-of-fact occurrences, with everything quite fair and aboveboard, those moments, so precious when they are stolen, might seem rather a waste of time than otherwise. I assume it to be a fact, that we value an article in proportion to the trouble or the time we expend in obtaining it, and do not estimate it at its intrinsic worth. I think it is quite possible that that gallant young adventurer, Leander, would not have been so devoted to his Hero, if he could have taken a return ticket per steamer across the Hellespont; and, for the same reason, I have no doubt that the shoulder of mutton and the bunch of turnips had an infinitely better flavour in the mouth of the fortunate and persevering chaw-bacon, who had become their rightful and proud possessor after the difficulties of a greasy pole, than if they had been procured in the ordinary way of business from the butcher and the greengrocer.

I am endeavouring, as my reader will see, I hope, to excuse the weakness and vanity of our little Priscilla—an inexperienced young thing in the wiles and the ways of the world, quite willing to love and be loved, and not knowing her own heart, profoundly ignorant of what may be lurking

in another person's, but believing every one possessed of a cultivated manner and gentle address,
to be as guileless as herself in thought and deed.
And this seems to me to be one of the difficulties
that innocence has to fight against in its contest
with the world; and I respectfully submit to you,
my dear madam, who would so carefully guard the
purity of your sweet child, by restricting him or
her as much as possible to your own and kindred
society, that you may quite unconsciously be preparing certain traps and pitfalls, which with a little
more knowledge of the world your precious treasure
might easily avoid, when your guiding hand is cold,
and your warning voice still for evermore.

I think, with this new excitement to occupy her
attention and please her fancy, Prissy would have
suppressed all mention of Mr. Sherwin's second
visit, if her father had chosen to keep silence on
the subject; but when Matthew returned that
evening—perhaps he had been considering the
matter for some reason of his own—he said,
brusquely—

" Has Mr. Sherwin been to-day ?"

Priscilla, blushing and confused, explained to her
father how Mr. Sherwin had been too late for the
previous evening's express train to London, and also
his intention, as he expressed it, of writing to him.
Her confusion was not relieved by the sharp pene-

trating look with which the old fellow met her,
when she ventured to steal a glance at him.

He continued silent for some time. The foul-
weather signals, which had become almost habitual
to his face, were more conspicuous than ever, and
he said, bluntly—

"Priscilla, this man is either a miserable sham,
or a designing knave—perhaps something of both.
If it was business that required him in town, he
could have taken a later train last night, or one
this morning. If he really desired to see me he
could have waited here, or called on me at my
place of business. His 'intention' of writing is a
puerile attempt to hoodwink me. I am heart-
sick and weary of the chicanery and hollowness of
the world. Have you any reason for supposing—
I expect the whole truth, mind—that he will
repeat his call to-morrow?"

"Oh no, papa!" Prissy exclaimed. "I am sure
he will not come again."

"Well," Matthew said, "we shall see."

No doubt Miss Priscilla was sincere at the
time; but whether she saw reason to alter her
opinion, or hoped it might not be a correct one,
certainly on the next day she had arranged her
dress to the best advantage, and was trilling her
little Italian song at the hour corresponding with
the time of Mr. Sherwin's call on the previous
afternoon.

At last a footstep was heard to approach the house, and stop at the door; and Miss Prissy's heart beat more quickly, and her colour heightened, as she awaited the now familiar knock;. but the door was opened, and her father entered. He darted a quick and comprehensive glance around, and then quietly went to the inner room and read the newspaper.

Thus, if Mr. Sherwin had only thought proper to defer his journey a second time, he might have had the interview he desired. But perhaps he had postponed the journey, and did not greatly desire the interview after all, for a gentleman, not unlike him in personal appearance—and that appearance was not a common one—saw from the further end of the street Mr. Worsdale enter the house, and he said—

" Devil take it !" as he turned the other way.

CHAPTER IV.

THE WILL—(AND THE WAY).

HILST the widow of that estimable Knight, whom envious persons were wont to call "Fishy Petitoe," was sunning herself one fine May morning in the neatly-kept garden of her trim villa at Broughton, and leaning on the friendly arm of her attached friend and companion, Miss Skimple, she confided to that judicious and sympathetic person her sufferings of the previous night. She had taken, so she believed, nothing unusual for supper, yet she thought she must have died before morning, such pangs had she endured. The sleepless hours, during which she had heard all the clocks in Manchester strike, her agony of mind and body, and her misgivings as to her probable tenure of life, had affected her spirits to that degree, that she owned to feeling "very low" and "ready to cry for nothing at all."

It was at a crisis like this that our dear Skimple proved herself to be the tender friend and skilful adviser that I think we have found her.

"My dear," that lady said, "it is probably a fit of indigestion—nothing more; you know, dear, I begged and prayed you not to touch the lobster. We cannot be too careful. You are of a delicate constitution—a breath may be too much for you."

"Oh, my dear, my dear!" Lady Petitoe exclaimed, beginning to shed tears; "do you think I shall die?"

"Indeed, I trust not," Miss Skimple replied; "though a person, whose life has been one of usefulness and unobtrusive Christian charity, may look towards the inevitable end without fear. Still you owe it to yourself, and those attached friends around you, to take every precaution possible."

"How do you mean, ' precaution?'" the lady nervously inquired; "you know I am never without my dinner pills—or my podophyllin."

"Yes, my dear," Miss Skimple replied, seating herself on a garden chair, while her friend endeavoured to recover her breath, which seemed somewhat uncertain and spasmodic; "but there are other duties and precautions that I refer to."

"I am sure," Lady Petitoe said, wiping her red and pale blue eyes, "I have endeavoured to walk uprightly in the tabernacle. I know I am a sinner —we are all sinners—but I trust——"

And here the worthy lady quoted several well-worn phrases of humility and self-abasement,

which are very popular with that class of preachers
who select corners of streets or waste grounds, or
any open place adapted for the exercise of their
peculiar powers; and which forms of speech, without being very intelligible to ordinary minds, are
nevertheless very effective in sound, and may be
acquired without much difficulty.

" Yes, yes, my dear, I *know!*" Miss Skimple
replied with some acerbity of manner—perhaps
she had heard these remarks before, and had
come to know them by heart. " I *know*. But
there are other duties; have you considered your
affairs ?"

This extremely practical and mundane question
seemed to startle Lady Petitoe, for she turned
suddenly round to her companion, and said—

" Whatever do you mean ?"

" I mean," said the stately Skimple, calmly and
deliberately, " that a person, blest as you are, my
dear, with affluence, and surrounded by every comfort that can bind the erring heart to sublunary
things, should consider well the disposal of her
worldly goods against the time when she will be no
longer able to enjoy them."

" I have never thought of that !" Lady Petitoe
said, looking aghast. " I thought Sir Septimus's
will would have settled all that ?"

" For your lifetime, dear, yes, no doubt," her

friend replied ; " but afterwards ?   I do not know—
nor do I seek to do," Miss Skimple continued, with
that calm air of superiority to all worldly considera-
tions that so well became her, " what the terms of
Sir Septimus's will were ; but it is right you should
be acquainted with it thoroughly.   You may have
some affectionate relative—or attached friend—to
whom you might wish to leave some tender memento
of yourself.   Have you thought of this ?"

"My dear Letitia !" Lady Petitoe exclaimed,
" it has never once occurred to me !   What ought
I to do ?"

" My dear," Miss Skimple continued, " it is not
for me in my position to direct your actions, or
to suggest you have been unconsciously neglectful
of relatives and friends, but a duty like that should
not be delayed."

" We will go at once !" her ladyship said ; " let
John get the brougham, and drive us to Mr.
Spink's office."

" My dear friend," Miss Skimple, firmly but
kindly, said, " you must not—you shall not—excite
or fatigue yourself.   In your present state of health
excitement would be highly dangerous, and perhaps
increase your already severe attack of dyspepsia.
Now, you know," she added, smiling grimly, and
becoming almost playful, if such a self-contained
and eminently circumspect lady could ever descend

to such frivolity, " I must have my own way here for once.   We will take a little light luncheon at one o'clock, and drive to your solicitor's in the afternoon."

And Miss Skimple had her own way.   Indeed, the domestics of that trim little villa used to say she always had her own way; and, in consequence, more than one had inquired, in a seditious tone, how many missuses she was to have?   At such indications of feeble rebellion our Skimple would turn rather yellow, perhaps, but she said nothing— and had her own way.

When the time came for setting forth, with that delicacy and high-breeding that more than anything distinguished her, she begged to be excused from accompanying her dear friend to the solicitor's; the business being, as she properly put it, of too private a nature for the presence of a third person; but as in proportion to her reluctance Lady Petitoe's requests arose to entreaty, she eventually consented, and the two ladies were accordingly driven to Mr. Spink's office that afternoon.

At the corner of the street in which the solicitor's office was situated, Mr. Rawley Todd—who had by this time developed into a showily-dressed young man, with a preference for strongly contrasted colours, and a perennially blooming flower in his buttonhole—was in earnest conversation

with his friend Tim Worsdale. From his fidgety
manner, and the uneasy glances he cast around, he
appeared anxious to terminate the conference;
whilst Mr. Tim hooking a finger in an unoccupied
buttonhole of the other's coat, seemed equally
desirous to prolong it. In fact, the unfortunate
Tim was suff'ering from a complaint that had become chronic with him, but which he was pleased
to call "only a temporary pressure," and he was
urging his former companion and fellow-student to
assist him with a trifling advance.

Mr. Rawley Todd was, as we have seen, of a
good-natured and compliant turn, but, as he assured
Tim, there was reason in everything, even to the
roasting of eggs, and beyond a certain figure he did
not feel justified in going. That limit, it seemed,
had been long since reached, and he felt reluctantly
compelled, as he said, in common justice to his
tradesmen, to decline opening fresh negotiations.

He was sorry to remind Tim of former obligations, but there was still a trifling matter of three
pounds which had never been liquidated, besides
other sums of a less amount which from time to
time he had been induced to advance. Tim, on his
side, admitted he felt hurt and humiliated, on his
friend's account, not his own (since the best of us
were liable to misfortunes), by this allusion; and he
didn't think that the Rawley Todd, by whose side

he had sat many a time in the happy old days,
would have been the party to throw undeserved
reverses into his teeth.   Mr. Todd, on the other
hand, asked his friend if he remembered when, in
the happy days referred to, he had been "short
of ochre," whose was the ready purse that was ever
open to meet the requirements of the hour?   If he
had forgotten who the party was who had always
said, " Tim, old man, if a pound will do it, say the
word?" and also the spirit in which that generous
confidence had been requited?   These questions,
put forward in an injured tone, had been met and
parried by other questions on Tim's side, as to
whether his liabilities had not been grappled with
in a straightforward and manly way, until undeserved reverses had crushed his heart out of him?
And this again naturally called up another pointed
question from Mr. Todd; for when an altercation
assumes this interrogatory form, so favourable to
the statement of personal grievances, there is no
telling when it will terminate; and it is possible
that one question would have continued to call up
another, until they had become grey-headed men,
or had been arrested for causing an obstruction in
the thoroughfare, if Lady Petitoe's carriage, stop-
ping at the office-door, had not afforded Mr. Todd
an opportunity to escape by hastening to assist her
ladyship from the vehicle; while Mr. Tim Wors-

dale, recognising in Miss Skimple a former acquaintance, who was never very favourably disposed to himself, turned on his heel and strolled carelessly in the other direction.

But in spite of the easy bearing he assumed, Mr. Tim's reflections on the hollowness of the world and the ingratitude of man were of the most bitter description. For it is the nature of improvident and worthless persons that they seldom recognise their own culpability, but ascribe to the hostility of others or the adverseness of Fate what is simply the outcome of their own deficiencies. So Mr. Tim Worsdale wended his way towards the small office he was wont to call his " place of business," brooding over his wrongs as he walked, and occasionally soliloquising in such fragmentary sentences as, " I didn't expect this of Rawley ;" or, " The world, sir, the world !" and other misanthropical utterances.

The relief that Mr. Todd felt at this unexpected means of deliverance from the importunities of Tim was so great, that it took the form of extreme cordiality and excessive politeness to the two ladies, and to such an extent, that Lady Petitoe expressed audibly her satisfaction with his attentions ; while the more observant Skimple mentally attributed them to an undue licence during the dinner hour, or possibly to an ulterior view toward Lady Petitoe's circumstances.

Having been duly introduced into the conference
between the solicitor and his client, Miss Skimple
was necessitated to hear a good deal of the disposition of the property by the will of the late Sir
Septimus.   I daresay many of the clauses and
technical expressions were not in the least com-
prehended by the disconsolate widow, who wept
copiously—I don't know why, but there are some
ladies who under such circumstances seem to confound bewilderment with grief,—but there was very
little that was not thoroughly mastered by her
friend.   Thus, in spite of the sighs and even sobs
of her sensitive ladyship, Miss Skimple learnt that,
beside the greater portion of his personalty, the
freehold of the Broughton villa was left by the
testator absolutely to his widow.

"My dear," Miss Skimple remarked as the
brougham was turned homewards, and her ladyship, having sniffed at some aromatic vinegar,
confessed she felt better, " you have acted most
judiciously and properly; and you see now, I am
sure, the importance of making some suitable disposition of your property."

"I am glad to think, Letitia," Lady Petitoe
replied complacently, "that it is so.   It has caused
me to feel in a truly Christian frame of mind.   I
think if John was to drive round by some of the
low parts of the town, we might do a little good by

leaving a few tracts and leaflets. I have some with me."

But Miss Skimple promptly reminded her that an epidemic was said to have broken out in those districts, and that the intention of the excellent society, that had for its object the amelioration of the struggling poor, would be equally well met if the little publications were left in the waiting-rooms of the railway stations, and such places, where the existence of malignant fever was not so probable. Lady Petitoe murmured something with reference to suffering for righteousness' sake, but either the reflection did not reach the ears of Miss Skimple, or she did not admit the cogency of it; for she directed John to drive round by the Victoria Station on his way home.

I do not know whether Miss Skimple considered that persons of the better class were in more need than their humbler fellows of such wholesome stimulus as was provided by the tracts and leaflets with which she was supplied by her friend, but leaving Lady Petitoe reclining in the comfortable brougham, and enjoying the Christian frame of mind of which she had spoken, Miss Skimple, avoiding the dirty floors and rough company of the inferior waiting-rooms, made her way to the more comfortable apartments appropriated to first-class passengers.

Having distributed on the table some little publi-

cations with suitable titles, such as " Where are you
going?" " The end of the journey," and " No return
ticket," she was about to retire, when she noticed,
seated in the corner of the room, Mr. Edward
Sherwin, apparently engaged in studying a time-
table. He evidently recognised her, she thought,
though he pretended to be so absorbed, and again
she felt that unaccountable embarrassment which
his presence had always caused. She withdrew,
however, apparently unseen, and having taken her
seat beside her amiable friend, was just saying, in
her usual harsh voice, to the driver, " Home,"
when a young girl, with long fair hair and pretty
blue eyes, turning into the doorway of the station,
paused for a few moments, looking earnestly at her.
But Miss Skimple did not seem to notice her, and
the girl, colouring deeply, turned away. Miss
Skimple, as we know, was not given to speaking
her thoughts as they arose in her mind, as many
weak persons, and even as her friend Lady Petitoe
was accustomed to do ; but had she uttered what
at that moment was passing beneath that cold and
placid brow, over which the hair of some one else
was so smoothly parted, she would probably have
said in the hasty and confused current the thoughts
often take—

" Priscilla is much grown—what is she doing
at that station ?—and Mr. Sherwin, or Captain

Clarence, or any other name that may answer his purpose—waiting in that room—and looking at a time-table he wasn't reading—pretending not to see me—a very suitable place for an assignation, no doubt—it would be only right to put Mr. Worsdale on his guard—I don't know where they live—and don't want to—why should I—what will be the end of it, I wonder?—why does that man, with his white hair and evil eyes, make me feel so wretched when I see him?—and that pert Dolly, too, whom I could never understand—and, dear me! here's this stupid old woman by my side, with all the vulgar pride that a full purse gives, and no more brains than that cushion—who over-eats and over-drinks herself, too, at times—I do wish she would sit still, and not fidget about so—and clear her throat and breathe freely—a most unpleasant old person, to be sure!—with all the comforts of life ready made—and I!—Ah!—what a world it is!—we are taught to believe in the justice of Heaven!—well, well, it might be worse, but it is hard to feel so lonely—so lonely—Oh! so lonely!   Ah!"

"Ain't you well, dear?" Lady Petitoe asked, aroused by the deep sigh that terminated these reflections on the part of her friend, during which, I daresay, the poor soul had travelled back many miles on the road of memory, to days when the world had seemed as sunny and as bright as the happy face and the clear blue eyes of the girl she had just seen.

Miss Skimple smiled sweetly in return, and surmised that an early cup of tea would be pleasant and refreshing after the unusual exertions of the day. Lady Petitoe acquiesced with a suitable platitude, on the enjoyment by a well-regulated mind of well-earned repose, and leaned back again in her carriage as if with a view of testing its pleasures, quite unconscious how she had been the object of her attached friend's thoughts a moment or two previously.

If we could only know what our attached friends and affectionate relatives really think of us, perhaps we should pause before we told our favourite story again, or repeated our last witticism. We might suppress the account of that smart stroke of business, that successful interview, or that severe rejoinder, if we could only rightly interpret that twinkle in the eye with which we credit our vivacious account, when it is really an involuntary discount off our veracity on the part of the hearer. We young folks flatter ourselves we have hoodwinked our parents in the matter of that little bill, or the presentable young gentleman round the corner, till some fine morning we are fairly taxed with our little deceptions, and we find that we have been blind, not they. In after years, when we

have youngsters of our own, we moralise and ser-
monise, and warn them from the shoals and quick-
sands of life; but if we only knew the variety and
extent of their knowledge, the books they have
read, and how they are smiling in their sleeves
at our simple confidence in their innocence, we
should save ourselves the trouble. And how little
our dearest friends and intimates suspect what we
think of them! I suppose everybody has experienced that miserable tingling of shame when
some respected friend is making a fool of himself,
and we have either no opportunity, or we lack the
honest courage, to beg him to desist. What would
we not give for his sake, if he knew our sentiments
at such a moment! I imagine that women, with
their quick instincts and sensitive organisation, must
surely suffer a very martyrdom at times, unless their
admiration for the lords of their hearts amounts to
a fanaticism. If a man sometimes seems a fool in
the eyes of his friend, what must frequently be his
wife's opinion of him?

I have no doubt Michal was very proud of the
love of his majesty, King David, and perhaps
willingly condoned many little royal errors of conduct; very likely she loved to dwell on the resolute
daring of the youthful hero that smote the giant
champion of the enemies of her people, and that
she listened with rapture to his passionate love-

songs and his tender lamentation over his dead friend; but when, in a thoughtless moment, he insisted on dancing at the head of a procession, and that, too, in the scantiest of garments, we have it on authority that she turned from the window and despised him in her heart.

That same evening Matthew Worsdale was seated in his little room reading the paper. He had grumbled somewhat, when he found on his return that his little housekeeper was absent, and had left the house and himself to the care of an occasional assistant, who on certain days of the week was engaged to lighten Miss Priscilla's duties. Perhaps he could not avoid recollecting the days when his every wish had been forestalled, and his slightest requirement carefully considered, by the poor girl whom he felt he had driven from home. Where was she now, he thought? Why did she not write to him—forgetting that, as his own child, she might inherit something of his own stubborn spirit, under a sense of wrong or injustice? Miss Priscilla, on her return, had endeavoured to avert her father's anger, by accounting for her absence on the ground of having to make some necessary purchases for the house and having been detained. I do not suppose she thought it was imperative to add that she had been listening to the whispered love-words of her

mysterious admirer, nor did her conscience revolt
from such equivocation as her ingenuity suggested, in
order to escape from her father's questions.   But she
was not at peace for all that.   Deceit was not quite
new to her—perhaps it is natural to some young
folks; but this was deception in a new form, and
she had not yet become familiar with it.   She
looked at the sturdy old face before her, with the
heavily-knit brows bent over the paper he was
reading, and something in its earnest expression, or
from one of those subtle associations we are puzzled
to account for, her thoughts recurred to Dolly.   It
might be that she thought how that gentle and
honest face, with the calm, true eyes, contrasted with
the dangerous fascination of the voice and figure
to which her wayward thoughts would turn, and
that, so thinking, she felt its pure influence stealing
over her, for her own troubled brow grew smooth
again, while the tears rolled silently down her own
fair, young face.   Or it might be only the reaction of
some recent excitement—an emotion to which young
people are mostly subject; but whatever it was,
some unusual impulse of affection or regret affected
her, for moving softly towards her father, she
gently wound her arm around his neck, and
whispered—

"I am very sorry I was out, dear.   I wont leave
you again."

The old man laid down his paper, and pressing the fair young face against his own careworn and furrowed cheek, said gently—

"No, my darling, you must not leave me. I have only one daughter now."

The old man's simple faith in her, his reliance on her truth and affection, smote her far more deeply than his reproaches for her deceit would have done; her conduct had never seemed so utterly unworthy as now, and she hung upon his neck and sobbed aloud.

He caressed her and spoke words of comfort and kindness, and she could almost have fallen at his feet, and hiding her face, have confessed her falsehood on her knees; and yet she dared not, as if some stronger will than her own had interposed and held her back. And so, while her father spoke gentle and loving words, such as she had not heard from him for many a day, patting her head and tenderly smoothing the long soft hair, the evil influence prevailed, and she kept the secret of her falsehood to herself.

About the same hour Mr. Sherwin—or Captain Clarence—stood in the doorway of his hotel, and said softly to himself—

"I think the girl's infatuated me! I can't get the little witch out of my head."

The rich light of the sinking sun denoted the

closing hours of the bright spring day, as our dear Skimple looked into the pleasant garden, and in her own mind sentimentally compared that placid evening with the final closing of a bright and happy life, where the cherished objects of hope and toil have been obtained, and the toilers, watching the long shadows as they creep onwards, wait with calmness for the inevitable night.

A thrush that all through the long and trying winter, when hunger and stress of weather had made him unwontedly bold, had escaped the hostile intentions of young Manchester and Salford, was singing a joyous *capriccio* from the leading bough of a lofty elm; the staid domestic cat, basking in the warm evening sunlight and blinking her green eyes, was listening placidly to the music, and probably calculating the chances, if she were to scale the tree, with a view to a nearer acquaintance with the minstrel; while a little ordinary sparrow, hopping on the ground—but keeping a bright and wary eye on the domestic cat—was collecting materials for repairing his home in the eaves, which had suffered somewhat from the increasing bulk or the turbulent nature of his offspring. Peace and goodwill; comfort, plenty, individual security, and mutual trust (limited), were suggested by the familiar objects and the pleasant scenes they helped to animate. Lady Petitoe at this moment entered the dining-room, and advancing to the window where Miss Skimple was standing, placed her arm affectionately around the waist of her friend. Lady Petitoe had dined, and her eye was moist, and she said in the familiar husky voice—

"My dear, I have been thinking it all over again. I shall leave you this house in my will, and perhaps something else besides."

Miss Skimple turned a gratified look on her friend and smiled. At the same moment the thrush on the elm-tree thought proper to moult a small brown feather, which was immediately secured for repairing purposes, by the ever-watchful and indefatigable sparrow ; a circumstance remarked by the philosophical and observant cat, for she purred softly and turned a green eye towards the window where Miss Skimple was standing, reflecting possibly that, though long past the usual hour to commence building, it is never too late, in this world—to feather our nest.

CHAPTER V.

MAJOR MAISMORE AT HOME.

 HEAVY thunderstorm had broken over London on the evening when Major Maismore (as Frank Ossett knew him) had returned to town. The tempest had been brief but violent, and the heavy downpour of the rain had been accompanied by vivid flashes and terrible peals of thunder. The Major sat in his pleasant drawing-room at Bayswater, and opposite to him was the lady whose bright dark eyes had attracted young Ossett's admiration at Brighton. The violence of the storm had passed, but the heavy dropping from the eaves, and the intermittent rumbling of the thunder, bore evidence of the conflict that had been waging. Something of the fury of the elements must have found its way into that well-appointed apartment, for the bright eyes of the lady glistened with tears, and an occasional reproach broke from her pale lips and compressed mouth. The Major was quietly smoking his cigar, but his pale face, suppressed voice, and a certain fiery spark in his own

dark and small eyes, seemed to imply some violent
passion held in check, but not subdued.

Those eyes that narrow and grow darker in their
wrath, when the lips lose their colour and the voice
comes in husky whispers, may be used as beacons if
we care to mind them, to warn us from the whirl-
pools and the dangerous depths of human nature.
The vehemence of the thunderstorm, appalling in its
sudden fury, oftentimes sounds more terrible than
it really is; but there is a deep meaning in
the silent flow of the dark river, with its tiny
eddies and sullen ripples, that hints at secrecy and
death.

There had been a dispute between them, a serious
one as it seemed, with some bitter reproaches on
the lady's part, aggravated by the Major's self-
control; but the domestic storm was only lulled, not
laid at rest, for after a longer pause than usual her
tears rushed forth again, and she cried aloud—

" My God! that I could forget! Oh, that I could !"

(And it might be observed that though she spoke
English singularly well, and with less of the accent
than most of her country people, and adopted it too
on ordinary occasions, yet in the excitement of
anger she employed her native tongue, and uttered
her reproaches and regrets with the strong volubi-
lity the French can command.)

" Ah !" she continued, " why did I meet with

you ! why listen to you ! I had better have been the poor girl ! My life, what has it been ! A lie a cheat ! a snare ! No better—a snare !"

" My child," the Major said calmly as usual, but in the whispered voice, and with the glitter in his dark eyes, " regrets are useless. Fate ordained it otherwise. You were not born to remain a poor girl. You were by nature and disposition admirably adapted for——"

" Hah !" she cried, glaring with a very mischievous look in her handsome face.

" For what you are, my child," the Major replied quietly, but glancing rapidly and almost suspiciously at the fierce woman before him—they were seated over their wine, and a small dessert-knife lay on the table near her hand, a prettily-fashioned thing and little better than a toy for any practical purposes ; but the Major took it, and after balancing it, carelessly as it were on his finger, as he spoke slowly and calmly, placed it on the other side—" for what you are,—my helpmeet, my comrade, my other self ! What have you to forget ? You made your choice. I have not given you social position ; well, what then ? Would you have obtained it without me ? But you have had comforts and luxuries, things which are not to be acquired by merely asking. These advantages, however, you set at nought, and seem to remember nothing but the idle gossip of a stupid lad, whose foolish dinner talk aroused your jealousy."

" My jealousy !" the lady exclaimed.

" I said your jealousy, my child,". the Major replied, quietly as before.

She looked at him fiercely, but said nothing for some time. Then, as if she had been recalling the circumstance the Major had referred to—

" Mr. Ossett, he is a gentleman !" she exclaimed.

" He is," the Major rejoined, " and a young one ; otherwise you and I should scarcely have had the privilege of his acquaintance."

" Speak for yourself, if you please !" the lady said.

" I speak for both," he answered ; " we were both interested."

" Then why did we leave our other place ?" she asked ; " and why, I ask, do you never see him ?"

The Major paused a second, and then said with a touch of sarcasm in his voice—

" He has acqaintances I do not approve of."

" Are they too clever or too poor ?" she asked.

" I do not approve of," the Major continued ; " but," he said pleasantly, though he seemed to watch narrowly the effect of his words, " I said we were both interested, and your views may be different. I can supply you with his address, for I have his card in my desk."

" Do you intend to renew the acquaintance ?" she asked.

" I don't know," the Major answered. " Do you ?"

For a moment their eyes met;—her look somewhat puzzled, but open and inquiring; the expression of his own was wary and searching.

After this they sat a long time in silence, deeply engaged by their own thoughts. Suddenly the lady rose and said—

" I am going to retire now."

" It is quite early," the Major answered, " not more than ten o'clock."

" I am going to retire now," she repeated, and left the room.

The Major had taken up a paper and was apparently reading, but when he was left to himself the paper slid from his hands, and he sat motionless, thinking—thinking. Whatever his thoughts might have been he did not look younger or happier under their influence. Men who elect to lead the hard life of an adventurer, the hard life with the pleasant surroundings, a life of uncertanty and suspicion, would not be seen at their best when seen alone. In the masquerade of such an existence, the visor and domino become so habitual, that they are worn to some extent even before their most intimate fellow masqueraders; it is only in solitude when they drop the

loose robe that hides the ordinary attire, and lay the
mask on the table, that the patches and the wrinkles
may be seen. The Major lit another cigar, and then
took out his writing-desk. After searching a little
time he found an address card with the name, " Mr.
Frank Ossett," engraved, and his place of residence
added in pencil at the back. This he placed on
the mantelpiece, and seating himself at the desk
wrote a long letter, which he read carefully over
when completed, and placed in a pocket-book he
always carried with him. Then he wrote another
letter, but he sat with it in his hand awhile, as if in
doubt, and finally burnt it, carefully watching the
last spark die out, before he said, almost aloud—

" No, I'll give her another day or two."

Lighting a candle, as if for the purpose of retiring
to rest, another thought seemed to strike him, for
he paused and sat down to think again. Then he
drew back the window-curtain and softly pulled
down the sash, and, with the air of the summer
night blowing freshly, he lay down on the couch.

" Ha," he said, " I'll sleep here to-night. It will
be cooler, and"—he paused a second—" safer."

But a night spent on a sofa in the clothes which
have been worn during the day, does not afford a
satisfying rest. So the Major found, for it was
long before he could lose himself in slumber, and
then only for brief and irritating periods. His

slumbers were broken by unpleasant dreams, and more than once he started violently, and arose to see if the room-door was secured.

The lady, who complained of headache the next morning, and whose darkened eyes and feverish pulse denoted a restless night on her part as well, took a late breakfast in her chamber, and the Major soon afterwards left the house.

When he returned in the afternoon, he learnt she had arisen shortly after his departure in the morning, and having sent the servant for a cab, had also gone out and had not yet returned. He looked on the mantelpiece, and observed the address card of Frank Ossett had been taken away.

"By all means, my child," he said; "please yourself, and you will please me."

He rang the bell.

"Did Mrs. Maismore say at what time she would return?" he asked.

The servant said she had left no directions about the dinner-hour, and assumed she would be in by the usual time—six.

"That will suit me very well," the Major said; so he strolled quietly out, and calling a cab, desired to be driven to Frank Ossett's apartments in Seymour Street.

"He will be at his office about this time, I take it," he thought, as the cab stopped at the door.

It was as he had anticipated. Mr. Ossett had not returned, and was rarely in before the evening, the girl said; but would he leave his name or any message—or call again?

The gentleman in the cab said it was of no importance; he just called before leaving town; and the girl noticed he wore a travelling-cap, which concealed the white hair that made his appearance otherwise somewhat remarkable.

Did the girl know, he asked, whether Mr. Ossett's mother or sisters were in town—as he should much like to have seen them; "but, of course," he added, "you wouldn't know them—no, no."

"Please to wait a minute," the girl said, "and I'll ask."

She went into the house, and returning in a few minutes, said, "The mistress didn't know who it was, but a lady had called to-day to see Mr. Ossett."

"No doubt one of his sisters or mother," he said. "Did she leave her name?"

At this point the landlady appeared, and from her the Major learnt the lady visitor could scarcely have been Mr. Ossett's mother, not anything like old enough; and, moreover, spoke something like a foreign person.

"Ah, probably the French governess—quite

right. Thank you, very much ! Drive back,
cabman."

And closing the cab-door, the Major exchanged
his cap for his ordinary hat, and discharging the
cab at the gate of Kensington Gardens, walked
slowly on the pathway through the trees. It was
some time before he found a seat unoccupied at that
hour of the afternoon. At last in an unfrequented
part he lighted his cigar, and let his reflections
have free way.

" What is the move, I wonder ?" he thought ;
" has she been there before ? If she meets the
other fellow, there will be the devil to pay ! However, that's her look out. She leads to my hand
exactly as I could wish—as she has always done—I
must say, and this time without knowing it. We
shall see—we shall see."

After awhile he arose, and walking slowly away,
said between his teeth and in a scarcely audible
voice—

" Hortense, my child, our partnership is drawing
towards a close."

The lady had been in the house some time, he
learnt, when he returned home. She met him with
her accustomed smile, and her face had recovered
from the jaded and wearied look it had worn in the
morning. No allusion was made to the previous
evening, and whatever thoughts each had of the

other, they kept them in their own breasts.   They
conversed on different subjects, and the Major was
as usual quite polite, and the lady on her part was
equally self-possessed ; but there were certain furtive
glances, and a sudden gravity of expression, when
each thought the other was not observing, which
denoted the masquerading dress, and neither seemed
to think it desirable to lay it for the present aside.
Indeed the Major's politeness extended even to his
feeding off those dishes only of which the lady par-
took, and to drinking wine from the decanter she
herself had chosen.

Mr. Frank Ossett was a good deal surprised when
he learnt the errand of the strange visitor in the
travelling-cap.

" Why," he said to the girl when she had told
him, " my mother is in Dalesford ; I had a letter
yesterday.   I have no sisters, and we never had a
French governess.   The man must be a fool, or it's
some mistake.   Any one else been, Mary ?"

" Yes, sir," said the girl, reddening a little,
though I don't know why she should have done
so ; " a lady."

" A lady !" Frank said, reddening in his turn ;
" what sort of a lady ?"

The girl described her as accurately as she could,
and added that she seemed an " outlandish sort of
person," meaning possibly a foreigner.

" Ah," said Frank carelessly, " another mistake I suppose—unless it's the French governess the other lunatic referred to."

And he was considerably nearer the mark than he suspected.

The following days were passed by the Major in the usual way. His avocations, whatever they might be, kept him rather late in the night, or early morning sometimes ; and once or twice the lady had been from home in the day time ; but there was peace, outwardly at least, between them, and there had been no recurrence of the storm of a few nights previously.

One morning, at their late breakfast, the Major said with some significance in his tone—

" My child, I expect a young—I may say, a very young—friend to dine with us this evening at six. It will be an occasion on which you should favour us with your presence. I should like our dinner to be rather a choice one."

" Your very young friend, do I know him ?" the lady asked.

" Not at present, I think," the Major replied. " He is extremely fresh, and altogether a charming young man."

The lady looked at him in a searching manner, but his face betrayed no more than his words conveyed.

Breakfast over, she said—

"I will see to this at once; we are late as it is."

"Whenever convenient to yourself," the Major said politely, and took up the morning paper.

"But it is not the greenhorn you suspect it is," he said to himself, when he heard the outer door close, and watched her elegantly-dressed figure crossing the street. "It is not he this time, my child, whom you are going now to warn from the impending peril!"

He thought a while, and reflected it was some distance to Seymour Street, and she could not be back for an hour. He went to the chamber and took a lady's writing desk from the drawers on which it had been placed. It was locked, but he took out his own keys and found one that fitted the lock with so little trouble that he might have known it to be a duplicate. He looked carefully among the papers it contained, apparently without success in the object of his search, for he was about to replace them when he saw what seemed the pass-book of a bank. He opened it and carefully examined the contents. It was in account with the name of "Hortense Sandier."

"A private purse, eh, my child?" he murmured. "Very prudent and proper, indeed. You have been realising on your jewels, I believe; I have not seen some of them lately."

He replaced the contents as nearly as possible as he had found them, and put the desk itself on the drawers whence he had taken it; and then dressing himself with his usual scrupulous care, left the house. He returned in due time with his young friend, at whose club he had called for the purpose. His guest was a perfectly well-dressed, harmless young fellow of four or five-and-twenty. There are a good many of the kind to be met with in society, I believe, and to members of the Major's profession may be found useful.

During the evening the friends played a few games at piquet or écarté, or some such pleasant pastime, whereby agreeable occupation is afforded to the mind, and money can be made to change hands easily; and what with the excellence of the Major's cigars, and the admirable quality of his wine, his young visitor spent a very pleasant evening.

The lady, who usually took so much interest in these friendly contests, seemed on this occasion so utterly indifferent and distraught, that the Major inquired with some asperity if she felt bored by their play, and would she prefer to retire?

It was in the small hours of the morning when the Major put his very young friend into a cab, giving his address to the driver, placing the fare in

8—2

his hand at the same time, and taking the number of the cab as he did so.

Two days after this, when the lady was absent from home, Major Maismore was driven away in a cab, with a large portmanteau on the roof, having previously left on the table a letter which he had taken from his pocket-book, and addressed to Mademoiselle Hortense Sandier.

CHAPTER VI.

ABOUT this time, Miss Priscilla Worsdale's habits underwent considerable change. We have known her as a young lady by no means remarkable for self-denial, industry, and early rising; but for some days past her grim old father had observed with satisfaction that every morning she had left her chamber, and made a show, at least, of setting the house in order by the time he appeared. I have no doubt he remarked in his own mind what a feeble little attempt at housewifery it was; but he gave her credit for good intentions, and was pleased accordingly. The general postman, engaged in the first morning delivery, soon recognised the pretty, blue-eyed and fair-haired young girl, awaiting with an anxious face his coming every morning; and more than once, when he had no letter to leave at Matthew Worsdale's house, he could not forbear his homely jest of "Nothing this morning, Miss. I'm afeard he's forgetting you," causing poor Prissy to retire

blushing and confused, while he, grinning at his
own humour, knocked at the next door.   Certain
it is, that official had never any occasion to knock
at Matthew's door, and once when Matthew had
said, in his usual curt way, " Any letters for me ?
I didn't hear the postman," his little daughter had
said, " Nothing, dear," and had turned away to
hide the confusion, which a letter, thrust hastily
inside the bosom of her dress, drove scarlet to her
face and neck—a letter she was longing to read,
and durst not, lest her father should observe it and
discover her falsehood ; and so she carried it about
with her, next to her weak and unsuspecting heart,
poor child, to prize and treasure, as fair and innocent women, before her time, had carried a poison-
flower, placed by a treacherous hand in their lover's
nosegay.

At last the hour struck at which her father left
home for his place of business. Prissy accompanied
him to the door, and kissed her hand prettily to
him as he left; and it pleased the old fellow,
though he forebore to acknowledge it, for he walked
down the street with something approaching a
smile on his furrowed face.   When he had turned
the corner, Prissy shot the bolt of the outer door,
and had taken the letter from her bosom, when Phil
called from the inner room—

" I say, Pris, where's Tim got to, do you think ?"

" Dear me, child !" the girl said, with some irritation. " How should I know ? In bed, I suppose."

" That he isn't," Phil said.   " And what's more,
he hasn't been in his bed all night.   I didn't like to
tell father ; he'd have gone on so."

" Good gracious !" Prissy said.   " I know nothing
of the boy ! He comes in and goes out pretty
much as he likes, I think !"

" Well, I tell you what it is, missis," Phil said
gravely.   " I should never be surprised at that
young man coming to grief."

" What do you mean, Phil ?" his sister asked.

" Well, never you mind," Phil said.   " It's no
use my talking to him.   He doesn't mind what I
say a bit !"

" I don't know what it means," Prissy said,
looking frightened.   " But it all seems very
dreadful !"

" Ah !" Phil said, as he put on his cap and
prepared to take his leave.   " It was different
when Dolly was here ! Poor old Dolly ! She could
always keep Tim in order, and never seemed to do
it neither !"

" Poor Dolly !" Prissy said, sitting down, and
letting her hands fall listlessly in her lap.

" Poor Dolly !" Phil said, sitting down also.
" I've a good mind to set off some morning, and look
for her.   I know if anybody could find her I could !"

"You wouldn't know where to go, Phil," Prissy said gravely, "or I should say go as soon as you can, and bring her home again; for no one feels her absence more than I! Poor, dear Dolly!"

There was more significance in the words as she spoke them than the boy could discern, for he sat simply looking before him, as if lost in his own reflections; while Prissy gave way to her grief, and wept. The thought of the dear absent one had aroused the pure affection of her nature, and she unconsciously placed her hand on her bosom, where the treacherous letter lay concealed like a venomous thing, coiled beneath the leaves of an innocent flower.

"Hollo!" Phil cried, as he perceived a corner of the letter peeping from her dress. "You haven't heard from her, and not told us, Pris, have you?"

"No!" the girl said, reddening. "It's nothing—nothing."

"Well, it's a letter, ain't it?" Phil asked.

"Never mind what it is! It doesn't belong to you, I suppose?" Prissy answered.

"All right, ma'am!" Phil said, going towards the door. "Don't fly out at me. There's no Act of Parliament against asking civil questions, I believe. I think I'll look in at the lock-up as I go by, and see if Tim's had a night's lodging there."

With which sarcasm Phil left home for the

business of the day, and, as usual with boys of his age, health, and temperament, whose grief, sincere and poignant as it may be, is soon succeeded by the sunshine of their genial natures, strove to beguile himself from his recent trouble of mind by whistling to the extent of his power such melodies as were then in vogue, or indulging in altercation with other boys, who, presuming on his inferior size, proceeded to personal liberties, or encroached on what he considered his rights. Left to herself, Prissy once more secured the outer door, and had once more taken the letter to peruse, when a heavy knock was heard.

"Dear me!" she cried aloud. "Whatever is it now?"

As she passed the window, she saw the figure of a man standing on the pavement; but he was so shabbily dressed, and seemed so dirty, and so suspicious-looking a character, that she wisely took the precaution of putting on the slip-chain before opening the door.

When the man said, in his coarse, rough voice, "Is Tim Worsdale in?" she recognised in him Mr. Thomas Stepper.

"Her brother was out," she replied, "nor did she know when he would return."

"I wanted to see him," Mr. Stepper explained. "I wanted to see him—bad."

But Prissy could only say he wasn't at home, and Mr. Stepper said—

" Well, take that there chain down, and let me in ; I've gotten some'at to tell thee."

But Prissy discreetly declined acceding to this proposal. Mr. Stepper's appearance was never prepossessing, and just now that worthy appeared to have suffered from those fluctuations of fortune to which all enterprising spirits are liable. His usual bullying expression when he had to deal with persons weaker than himself, had given way to a hang-dog, skulking look, that was still more revolting ; and his pale face, which had evidently been closely shaven, with his remarkably short crop of hair, seemed to imply a recent compulsory retirement from public life.

" I've been in trouble," he said briefly, as Prissy, with the door held ajar by the chain, waited to hear what he had to say.

" In trouble ?" the girl said, innocently supposing he was referring to some domestic affliction. " Is your wife ill, or children ?"

" Wife !" he exclaimed with a savage expletive. " It ain't that. Don't you know what trouble is ? I've been jugged."

Poor little Prissy, whose knowledge of her native tongue did not extend to the lingo employed by Mr. Stepper's fraternity, was at fault again. She had, in the days of their prosperity, known and partaken of certain savoury dishes, which it was customary to speak of as being " jugged," and that idea hastily or half-formed was foremost in her mind ; but she could not comprehend that process as applied to a human subject in a Christian country, and least of all his being in a position to speak of it.

" I am afraid," she said timidly, " I don't understand you."

" God's truth !" the ruffian exclaimed. " Well, then, I've been quodded—had two months in gaol Now do you know then ?"

" In gaol !" Prissy repeated.

" Ah, in gaol !" Mr. Stepper said. " Some one took and blowed on me, and I got nabbed ; and I'm bless'd"—(by the way, he didn't say " bless'd,' but I prefer to employ that word)—" if I don't think it's that there Tim what done it !"

" Tim did it ? Tim did what ?" Prissy asked.

" Why—*It*—blowed," Mr. Stepper said, raising his voice as his anger increased, " and if I catch hold on him I'll twist his neck like that there !" and from the vigorous turn he gave his wrist, and the spark of anger in his eye, Prissy had no doubt he would have been as good as his word.

" I see him two nights ago at the pub," Mr. Stepper proceeded to say, " an' when he spotted me he stepped it precious quick. I came round here and waited for him, but he never turned up—if he had !—if he only had—!"

And here Mr. Stepper's indignation became so violent, and he emphasised his language with so many evil adjectives and coarse oaths, that Prissy, to whom most of his foul words had fortunately no meaning beyond their dreadful sound, became quite frightened and begged him to go away.

" Go away ?" Mr. Stepper inquired, by way of opening up a new vein of complaints, " where to ? what's the use ? I haven't got a blessed mag, nor I haven't had no victuals for more than a day. Is that the proper way to treat a poor cove, as has been led away by such as him ? Blowed upon an' jugged ! Go away ! Where to ? Where the devil to ?"

Thoroughly frightened by his ruffianly violence, Prissy said timidly—

" I have no money in the house, Stepper."

" No money ? That wunnot do ! Where did she, the other one, get it from when I comed afore ?" he demanded.

" I have only half-a-crown of my own," she said— " I'll give you that if you go away."

" Half-a-crown !" he repeated in a tone of great disgust. " Well, where is it ?"

Prissy gave him the money, shuddering as her fingers touched his coarse and dirty palm.

" What's the good of this here to me ?" he asked.
" Han't you got no more than this ?"

" No, indeed ! None that I can get at," she
said. " Father always keeps his money locked up."

Mr. Stepper appeared to reflect for a few moments,
for he said, assuming the plaintive accents that professional mendicants know so well how to adopt—

" I've had nought to eat for hours and hours. If
you could stand a bit of bread an' cheese, I should
raly take it as a Christian kindness."

" Yes, Stepper," the girl said, " I can find you
that readily."

" Thank you kindly, good lady," the man said,
and seemed so grateful, that Prissy was truly glad
she could relieve suffering humanity so easily.

" An' a drink of beer, perhaps ?" Mr. Stepper
modestly suggested.

" I will see if we have any, if you'll wait," she said.

" I had better come inside, perhaps ?" Mr.
Stepper gently urged.

But Prissy didn't hear this last proposal, having
gone to the inner room for the cheese and the loaf.
Her attention was attracted, however, by a slight
rattling at the door, and she saw the coarse and
dirty hand had been softly introduced, and was
endeavouring to deftly remove the chain from its
fastening. This however was impracticable, the
shortness of the chain not admitting of the intro-

duction of the wrist and the removal of the catch
at the same time. She remained silent, becoming
more and more frightened, until she felt somewhat
reassured by the hand being withdrawn; but only
for a moment, for it directly afterwards appeared
again, holding a pocket-knife by the extreme end
of the haft, and with extended blade feeling for the
holdfast of the little slip chain. Then the full
danger of her situation struck her for the first
time. Unprotected and alone, what could she do,
even at that time of day, opposed to the strength
of a ruffian like that? Why, a blow would render
her helpless, and he could rifle the house at his
leisure! She uttered a short cry of terror and
sprang at the door, driving it with some force
against the fingers of the ingenious Mr. Stepper,
who howled aloud with pain, and remonstrated with
her for her violence, in a strain not to be easily
surpassed even in Pedlington. Finding, when he
heard her lock and bolt the door, that he had been
foiled, he struck the panel with his clenched fist,
and expressed his intention of kicking it in then
and there; but a policeman, whose duty was supposed to be to watch over that locality, and to
stroll occasionally down the street, happening to
turn the distant corner, Mr. Stepper, with many
strong references to his evil fortunes, and some
emphatic imprecations on the door, the house, the

family generally, and even himself, deemed it
advisable to walk the other way.

Left to herself once more, and having recovered
a little from the excitement, which so unusual an
occurrence in their quiet home had just occasioned,
Prissy sat down for the third time to peruse the
letter. She had recognised the handwriting of the
superscription at once, but was scarcely prepared for
such earnest and tender words as she read, delighted,
over and over again. It hinted at the difficulty
the writer had previously mentioned, in the objection he feared her father had begun to entertain so
unjustly towards himself, and he besought her in very
loving language to meet him that evening at their
usual trysting place, or, should that be impracticable
or inconvenient, he would, when all was still in the
night, make his way to the house, and that perhaps
his dearest girl would grant him a few moments'
interview, when her absence from home would not
be remarked.

Here was a proposal, romantic, mysterious, and,
as far as her father's knowledge of it was concerned,
dangerous, that pleased the fancy of the impulsive
young girl, and she sat silently thinking over the
fearful joy of such clandestine interviews, and calling to mind such incidents of a similar kind as she
had read or heard of.

We will not be too hard on her, if you please.

We will remember she is only a young girl and a
spoilt child, having experienced, with her family, a
sudden reverse of fortune—that she had no friend
or counsellor of her own sex; that her life was a
dreary and unpleasant one, and with these difficulties to contend with, and naturally of a weak and
pliant nature, she had been placed within the
dangerous influence of the stronger will of a more
evil nature. I am inclined to believe myself,
though what we call virtue and prudence are sometimes innate, or even inherited, that virtue is frequently only an accident of station, and prudence
oftentimes nearly akin to self-interest. The high
road of propriety, although level and straight, is
sometimes dry and dusty; and if in commencing
our journey we look aside on those pleasant pas-
tures (whereon, by the way, trespassers are inevit-
ably prosecuted and punished sooner or later), I do
not think it argues natural wickedness so much, as
the not unnatural curiosity for what is prohibited.
Perhaps, if those whose duty or pleasure it is to
teach us young things the path we ought to go,
would specify more plainly the dangers that surround
us, and not confine themselves to generalities, some
of the sins which may be imputed fairly to ignor-
ance, or even in some cases to innocence itself,
might be avoided, and that too without soiling the
purity and integrity of our teachers.

Our little Priscilla, who was simply a fair type of the ordinary class of girls in her station of life, with the good and the evil in her nature pretty equally balanced, and with nothing remarkable on either side, was sufficiently flattered and pleased by the glowing language of her lover's letter, and never strove to fathom its full meaning and intention; whilst she made ingenious excuses to herself for any deception she might deem it expedient to practise, or taxed her memory for precedents in filial deceit.

When her father returned home at the close of the day, Prissy, who had learnt the various expressions on his face, saw something had greatly disturbed him. The familiar foul-weather signals were conspicuous enough, but there was manifestly some great grief at the old man's heart, that he could not, or would not, disclose. Little Phil, in the exuberance of his animal spirits, had come jumping and whistling home, but was awed into respectful silence at the first glance.

And in constraint and silence the evening was passed, till close upon the time for retiring. Then Matthew said, with difficulty and in a husky voice—

"My children—Priscilla and Philip—it is a twelvemonth to-night since that terrible fire. The anniversary of such an event is a suitable occasion to receive this letter."

He took from his breast-pocket a letter addressed to him at his place of business, and said to Prissy—

"Read this, my dear. No," he continued, as if determined to overcome any weakness he might feel, "I will read it myself. It is from your brother."

He paused a few seconds, and then with knit brows and a steady voice, he read—

"DEAR AND HONOURED FATHER,—

"I write from Liverpool, but when you receive this I shall be far away. My troubles have been more than I could bear, and for some time past I have seriously entertained an idea of self-destruction, as the only means of relief from the continual financial pressure which it has been my hard lot to endure. I have been spared from the sin of rashly ranking myself with the dead, by the providential interposition of an unexpected friend. He it was who kindly pointed out to me the folly and the wickedness of such an act, and wisely reminded me that, living as we do in a civilised and a Christian country, my life was not my own, nor was it to be lightly thrown away. His arguments convinced me of the error of my ways, and yielding to the advice of my friend, who I may in truth term my second father—viz., Sergeant Romfitt, of the 97th Foot, who is recruiting here, I enlisted yesterday in his regiment (bounty £5), and the life which had been a burthen to self and friends, will be in future at the service of my sovereign and my country!"

The old fellow paused a moment or two—Phil and Prissy in open-eyed wonder; and Matthew said more to himself than to them—

"And thank God it's no worse! Now then," he added, "Phil and Priscilla listen to this."

He recommenced steadily enough, but his voice broke once or twice, and he was evidently suffering under some strong emotion, which he strove, but not quite successfully, to control; for the rest of Tim's letter was an admission of the unworthy share he had had in poor Dolly's disgrace and dismissal, and, as if whatever was false and sham, when it came under the influence of her truth and honesty, must acquire some worth from the association, the rhodomontade of the worthless lad's character seemed to drop out of the letter, as he endeavoured to clear her name and pleaded miserably for forgiveness. Prissy's sympathy and Phil's affectionate nature were easily aroused, but Matthew struggled bravely on to the concluding line, and then he gave way. I don't think he had any feeling of regret for his son, for he let fall his troubled face between his hands and sobbed—

" Dolly, my child ! my poor child ! And I believed myself a just man ! God forgive me ! Dolly, my poor child—my poor child !"

He had not read the whole of the letter before he told them, only the former part of it, which referred to his son. Tim's confession seemed to have plunged him in the deepest anguish, and more than once he groaned aloud. That keen discernment, in which he believed himself so strong, and his stern spirit, which from the long habit of years he had fancied almost infallible, had failed him when he most needed light and help, and he had never felt so much a bankrupt and a broken man as now. Perhaps a suspicion of his own injustice had not been wanting, and this night's letter had only confirmed his fears. It is a long time before certain strong and hardy natures bend under grief and trouble, but when they do at last yield, their utter prostration is the more terrible to see. So it was with Matthew Worsdale. He had difficulty even in making his way to his bedroom, and Prissy heard him moaning or sobbing when he thought she was asleep.

But she was not asleep. She was seated by the window, through which the bright moon shone so clearly that she could see to read the letter she had received in the morning. She had been so impressed by her father's sorrow that she had determined never to vex or to deceive him more, but having taken out the letter to put it far away out of sight —under lock and key—had yielded to the temptation to read it once more, and dwell on the pleasant words it contained.

Then her good resolution was shaken, and she thought for a minute or two how safely she might slip down the stairs, and open the house-door, as proposed in her lover's letter; even if it were only to say good-by, or to entreat him to see her father in the morning, and terminate this deception. Yes—she persuaded herself—that would be the better plan. It was the hour at which she might expect to see him, and perhaps a word or two from her own lips might have more effect than any written entreaties. So, with this conclusion, she unlocked a private drawer to place the letter among other little treasures she kept there, and her hand fell on the letter Dolly had written, part of which has been quoted.

In the still hour of the night, and in her present impressionable state of mind, Prissy took her sister's letter to read again, standing with her back towards the window that the moon's light might fall full on the paper.

When she had first received this letter, she had, in her sisterly love, placed inside the cover a likeness of Dolly herself, and now, holding this near

her bosom in innocent affection, once more read the
tender words that Dolly had written—

"Kiss dear father for me, Prissy; be good and
true to him, and tell him gently, with my love—
more love than he can ever know I feel—that he
has misjudged me—but———"

She could read no further. "Be good and true
to him"—these words had a meaning she had never
felt till now. "Tell him gently he has misjudged
me." Yes! he had misjudged Dolly—poor Dolly
—and she knew how the terrible truth had come
home to the old man that night. But had he not
also misjudged her? his favourite, his little petted
child, for whom nothing had been too good, and
whom he so loved and trusted? Did she deserve
that love and trust, standing there as she had been,
planning deceit and treachery? She looked again
at the little portrait, and Dolly's gentle eyes seemed
to look back into her own, and in simple, earnest
penitence she wept.

At that moment the figure of a man, partly in
shadow on the other side of the way, paused and
looked up at the window. She turned and they
saw each other, and he made a signal to her. But
it was in vain; the pure soul and the loyal heart
that had looked out of the little portrait in her
hand, and breathed through her sister's simple letter

the homely words of tenderness and love, triumphed over the evil influence without, and Prissy fell upon her knees, thanking God, and holding Dolly's portrait to her lips.

The figure outside waited some time, taking out his watch more than once. At last, with an expression of annoyance muttered from between his teeth, he turned away.

Another figure, bearing in its clumsy thick-set form a strong resemblance to the person of Mr. Stepper (lying in wait probably for the hapless Tim), and carrying a short heavy stick, came forth from a dark alley close by, and keeping well in the shadow, followed softly behind.

CHAPTER VII.

ROSEDALE.

PRISSY received no more letters; and having waited one or two mornings with a strange sense of relief, not unmixed perhaps with a little womanly pique, she concluded all communication was over between them. The jocular postman missed the pretty and anxious face he had become accustomed to look for standing at her father's door awaiting his coming; and when he next brought a letter for Mr. Worsdale he said, as he delivered it into Prissy's hands—

"He's quite forgot you, Miss, I do think! He don't deserve his good fortin', do he?"

And so he went grinning on his way, dealing out his tidings of good and evil at the various doors, as the card-player scatters his little heaps of paint and pasteboard that bring us fortune or hasten our ruin. Matthew, as his custom always was, read his letter to himself and placed it in his pocket, that he might afterwards communicate its contents or not as he thought proper. The last day or two had

worked a change in him, it seemed. He had a
more softened look, and his voice had become
gentler, and many little endearments of phrase and
manner which had long been laid aside returned to
him. Dolly's name had not been mentioned since
the night he had received the letter from his son,
but he had spoken once or twice of Tim, and with
more forbearance than might have been expected.
Perhaps he had learnt to mistrust his own discernment, and was reluctant to pass judgment as he
would have done some time ago. When he returned at his usual hour in the evening, he gave
Prissy the letter to read, which was as follows :—

" Raymond Buildings, Gray's Inn,
" July 21, 18—.

" DEAR SIR,—

"Our client, Mr. Edward Sherwin, will
feel obliged by your appointing a day of meeting
on which he may submit to you certain proposals
for rebuilding the premises formerly used as a Mill
and Storerooms by Messrs. Sherwin and Worsdale,
situated in Dalesford, and destroyed by fire on the
20th of July, 18—. We are instructed to say
further that he is anxious to renew the business as
commenced by his late father, Mr. Job Sherwin,
and carried on by him and yourself under the firm
as above. He suggests you should see him on
as early a date as practicable, and proposes you

should meet at his new residence, the Lodge, Rosedale, near Dalesford, as being nearer to Manchester,
and perhaps more convenient to yourself. Your
early attention to this, stating your own views, will
be esteemed a favour.

   " We are, Sir,

     " Your obedient servants,

      " TITHERADGE AND BURNLEY."

" Oh, papa !" Prissy exclaimed, " that is good
news !   You'll go, dear, wont you ?"

Matthew looked thoughtfully at the girl and
said—

"I don't understand it, Prissy.   This sudden
action on his part is hardly square with his previous
character and" (he paused a moment) " conduct."

" How do you mean, papa dear ?" she asked.

"If it is only a sudden impulse, as I suspect,"
Matthew said, " nothing may come of it ; nor would
it be desirable to be connected in business with a
man who acts so hastily in such important matters.
If it is not an impulse, why did he not mention it
before, and see me fairly face to face, instead of
seizing the opportunity of my absence from home,
and visiting my house in a clandestine and unworthy manner ?"

" Father," Prissy said, rising and putting her fair
arms round the old man's neck, " I will never see

Mr. Sherwin again without your knowledge and consent. I am very sorry I ever did."

" My darling," the old man said, in his softened voice, and kindly taking her head between his hands, " I don't blame you. You are young, and know very little of the world—its many forms of knavery and the hollowness of its friendships; and if I could think you never would know them, I could die more happily. I know, my Prissy, you would not deceive me, and it is the entire trust I feel in you, that is some comfort to me now."

Prissy raised her face to his, but the blood had rushed crimson to it when she remembered her struggle with herself on the previous evening.

" Tell me truly—but I know you will, my dear," he said, " when did you hear from Mr. Sherwin last ?"

Deceit, however successful, has to pay a penalty at times, and this was an hour of reckoning heavy enough for Miss Priscilla. She was silent a little while, and more than one answer of that kind which without being directly false is not entirely true (in the form of prevarication, or an artful turn of the conversation, or some little blandishment that may divert the attention from the point—and all of which may be fairly reckoned among the accomplishments of some women), suggested itself to her; but after a little contest with herself, in which, I believe, a certain portrait and letter had something to do, she leant her head to her father's ear and whispered—

"Dear papa, I had his last letter two days ago."

A troubled look crept into the old man's face, and he was silent a moment or two.

"Priscilla," he said, gently but firmly, "will you show me that letter, my dear?"

"Yes!" she said; "I will fetch it now."

Matthew sat looking steadily before him in deep thought awaiting her return. She may have had another little struggle with herself, but she brought the letter and placed it in her father's hand. He read it over gravely more than once, and said—

"I need scarcely ask, Priscilla, if you have read this letter carefully?"

"Yes," she said.

"Many times, I daresay?" he added.

"Yes, father, many times," she answered, blushing.

"Do you think you understand it, my dear?" he asked.

"Yes, father. Why?" Prissy returned.

"Read, side by side, of the one I have received to-day," Matthew said, "I don't think I do, my child." He said, after awhile, "I shall return your letter in due time. I will see Mr. Sherwin as he proposes, and this letter must go with me."

Prissy looked surprised, but as Matthew refolded the letter and placed it in his breast-pocket, she remained silent.

Two days later Matthew Worsdale started on his journey to Rosedale, the residence of the son of his old friend.

Men like him have but little sentiment in their natures; if it ever existed, the battle of life, and the stern habit of many years of taking a simply practical view of things, crushes it out, or leaves it so little space to develop, that it is choked out of life by the more vigorous growth by its side. But, as the train in which he was travelling drew nearer to Dalesford, and the more familiar objects met his eye, he could not resist a feeling of depression and sadness. When the train reached that point of the line from which the blackened walls of the factory could be seen, he knit his heavy brows and compressed his lips, as a stout man does who sees an enemy approaching, and nerves himself for the contingency of a contest. Having waited for the allotted ten minutes at the Dalesford Station, during which Matthew sat back in the carriage with folded arms and a pale face, he was taken five or six miles further on, which brought him to the end of his journey. He had fallen into a deep reverie, and was aroused by a porter, or guard, calling out " Roddle !" with that strange propensity which

most of the order seem to have for rendering
unintelligible, as far as possible, the names of the
stations at which passengers may desire to alight.
Matthew, however, who took few things by hearsay
when he could have the evidence of his own eyes,
descried the name on the painted board near the
platform, and left the carriage. The place itself,
which served as a station for several circumjacent
villages, in which some of the branches of the staple
trade of Dalesford were carried on, was simply a
collection of a dozen or more tenements, occupied
by the operatives who found employment in the
Dalesford mills, and walked to and fro morning
and night, carrying in a pocket-handkerchief a
lump of bread, and perhaps a bone of meat, or a
slab of fat bacon to serve for dinner. The Lodge
was easily discernible—a stone building, of the
Elizabethan order, standing on an eminence, and
sheltered from the north and east by a lofty hill,
clothed with wood, at the rear. The aspect due
south commanded the pasture land on either side
of the little stream that flowed into Dalesford,
where it was duly contaminated by the refuse from
the mill works.

Matthew Worsdale stood in the doorway of the
roadside station, and pointing to the building, the
gables of which could be seen through the gaps of
the trees, said to the porter who took his ticket—

" That is Rosedale Lodge, I suppose?"

" Mr. Worsdale?" a man asked, dressed in the . quiet livery of a coachman as he advanced and touched his hat.

" My name is Worsdale," Matthew said.

" Master has sent the phaeton, if you will please to get in," the man said.

Then Matthew noticed the carriage with the stout bay horse, that was waiting at the door.

" No," he said, after a moment or two. " If that is the place I am going to, I can walk."

" The hill's rather heavy, sir," the man said.

" I prefer to walk," the old fellow said, and started at once.

I daresay he could not have explained the reason for his choice. It was a steep hill, as the man had said, and the road winding about to render the ascent less difficult, considerably lengthened the journey. Perhaps he wished to see the surroundings of the place, which he might have thought he could do better than by riding; perhaps, with characteristic obstinacy and pride, he would not commence the interview by accepting an obligation, small as it was. At nearly every bend of the winding road Matthew stopped and looked about him. On either side of the meadow land in the valley, the lofty hills stretched out into the far distance, varied and rich in the bright summer tints, and deep purple

shadows cast by the July sunshine. Arrived at the
gate of the Lodge, Matthew paused again. The
garden, with a short carriage-drive to the house-
door, was skilfully laid out and neatly kept. The
smoke and the noise, and the many abominations of
Dalesford, inseparable, I suppose, from a manufacturing locality, seemed shut out by the hill on the
north-east, and the place was a simply beautiful
English landscape, suggestive of peace, comfort, and
prosperity. We may find many spots like this in
the West Riding of Yorkshire, if we care to look for
them, where the rugged and the sublime in Nature
is softened down and beautified by the purely picturesque that lies nestling beside it. Matthew
drew a long breath of the soft southern breeze that
stole up from the verdant hollow, bringing with it
faint odours of the newly-stacked hay and the
fragrant wild flowers, and the old fellow's face
softened a little under the wholesome influence.
But the frown returned to his brow, and the lips
hardened themselves again, as he nervously felt for
the treacherous letter, with its smooth words of
flattery and love, as if to assure himself of its
safety. He had done this more than once on his
journey.

Perhaps, in his own mind, he had resolved before
any negotiations of business were commenced to
require an explanation. Why, he thought, could not

this man, united to him by old associations at least, have been fair and honest, as his good father would have been, and as he (Matthew) himself was ? Had he loved Matthew's little daughter purely and truly, why should he not have addressed her in the broad light of the day, under her father's own eyes, if not with his full concurrence, at least with his knowledge. He felt he would have been happy and proud to have seen her, in the proper time, the little mistress of that bright home, with the pure influence of God's beautiful country shielding and confirming her innocent nature.

" Bah !" he exclaimed in a tone of disgust, as he turned slowly on his heel, grinding down the gravel in the pathway as he did so. " The man's a knave ! a wretched piece of shoddy at the best; and if I can see him face to face, and tell him so, I shall not have had my journey for nothing."

As he walked slowly and firmly up the garden path to the house door he had a sense of anger and resentment coming over him, an almost rebellious feeling against the Providence that had made the path of life so pleasant for this worthless man, and had left it so rugged and so difficult for himself.

Then he went up the steps, and rang the bell loudly.

When the servant opened the door, he said bluntly—

"My name is Matthew Worsdale. I am here by appointment to meet Mr. Sherwin."

The servant conducted him into a cool and pleasant room, where a neat luncheon was prepared.

"My master will be with you directly, sir," the girl said ; "and will you please to take some refreshment ?"

"I am here to talk, not to eat," he replied roughly. "I have no desire to stay longer than is necessary. Let me see your master as soon as I can."

But he drank a glass of water to cool his parched throat, and sat down wearily in a chair. He scarcely noticed the pleasant room, or the lovely prospect from the window ; he was thinking of the sad changes of the past year, and the gloom that hung over it was too heavy for that bright summer sun to disperse. His home broken up, his fortunes bankrupt ; wounded, where he believed himself invulnerable ; deceived, where he had most faith, baffled and disappointed, he sat gloomily beating the floor with his heavy foot, his head bowed down and resting on the hand that concealed his sad and troubled face.

He had sat thus some little time thinking— thinking—and almost unconscious of what might be passing, when he felt the light touch and gentle pressure of a loving hand on his head, and stealing round his neck, and heard a soft and timid voice whisper in his ear—

" Father ?—dear father ?"

The old man started, and turning deathly pale, looked up and caught poor weeping Dolly to his heart; pressing her loving face to his breast, and saying reverently, " Thank God !" bent his head over her and wept.

And so they remained a while, Matthew pressing his lips on Dolly's head, and she kneeling at his feet and holding his right hand between her own. Then he felt the hand she held so tenderly was being placed within a stronger grasp, and another voice than Dolly's said—

" Side by side again, Matthew Worsdale; and please God, side by side to the end !"

" Joe Boothroyd !" Matthew cried, as he looked up.

" No, Matthew Worsdale ; Edward Sherwin, now and henceforth·; your old friend's son——"

" Let *me* tell him, Joe !" Dolly whispered, " my husband, father; my dear husband !"

The old man looked from one to another with a pained expression of doubt, and involuntarily placed his hand on the letter he had brought.

" It is a long story," Joe said, " and a sad, perhaps a foolish one ; even Dolly here has not heard the whole of it, but I will tell it faithfully, and you shall give me your hand, Matthew Worsdale, or withhold it, as you shall find I have striven to deal tenderly and justly by you and yours."

Matthew remained silent a few moments, looking narrowly and keenly under his heavy brows, then he said, but in subdued voice and apparently with difficulty—

" Mr. Boothroyd—I cannot help calling you by the name by which I have known you—I thank you for this meeting with my daughter, whom I know now I had misjudged and wronged ; and I am grateful for the assurance I have from her own lips in calling you her husband, that by your means she is placed in a home far better than any I could offer her. If I have ever misjudged and wronged you too, sir, I fairly ask your pardon as a man should do, who, trying to be just and to do right, miserably fails. I ask your pardon, and—and—I ask hers."

He paused again, and with a convulsive movement of the lips and throat, as if in the violent effort to check some strong emotion. Dolly putting her arms round his neck kissed him passionately, and whispered sobbing—

" Don't, dear father !—don't say that !"

Matthew put her on one side, though very gently, and went on—

" I am a broken man, Mr. Boothroyd, and I pray God to forgive the errors of my failing judgment.

Perhaps the suffering I have had may be the punishment he has allotted me. But you are not the man I have been led to believe was the son of my old friend. You are not the man who came to my house as Mr. Edward Sherwin, with letters and other evidence of his identity, and who professed affection for my younger child. It would be an intense relief to me, sir, to be assured—I say *assured*—that the man who could plan secret interviews, such as he proposed, and who could write this," (and here Matthew produced the letter), " was *not* my dear old friend's son, but an impostor and a cheat; and it would be only right to you and to myself to know why, if you are the man you say, you should have chosen the position of a servant, where you would have been recognised as a principal, and why you should have thought it wise and proper to have adopted the masquerade of name and manner to obtain a footing in my family, which the son of Job Sherwin might have claimed."

" Mr. Worsdale," Joe said, " I cannot blame you for your doubts; and I partly expected them. Before I tell you my story and attempt to explain the course I adopted, I should be glad if all your doubts could be set at rest. But there are many things I cannot account for, principally the possession by another person of the letters of my father that you refer to. I have a great difficulty in guessing how this person,

whoever he may be, became acquainted with the
circumstances of our connexion, and when or why
he first thought of availing himself of the knowledge of it. I hope this may be made clear before
we have done. In the meanwhile consider me still,
if you please, your old foreman, Joe Boothroyd—I
don't dislike the name, sir"—he looked kindly at
Dolly as he said it, " until you *are* assured I have a
just claim to another. I expect my solicitor, Mr.
Titheradge, from London, in about half an hour's
time, and we will, if you please, suspend our business
until his arrival. But let us, in the meantime, prevail
on you to take some rest and some refreshment."

But Matthew Worsdale could not eat nor rest.
He placed the letter he had brought with him in
Joe Boothroyd's hand, but without saying a word,
and paced the room with a troubled face, looking
sometimes at his watch, or gazing wistfully out of
the window, and beating his foot nervously on the
floor. Once or twice Dolly tried to rouse him by
asking about Prissy or little Phil. But his answers
were short and to the point, and she knew him too
well in these moods to try him further.

" I need scarcely tell you," Joe said, after reading
the letter Matthew had handed to him, " that this
was never written by me. I assume that you are as
well satisfied on that point as that the man calling
himself Edward Sherwin, and whom you have fre-

quently seen, and I are two persons. There can
be no doubt we have both been the .victims of
some ingenious scoundrel, and, reading this letter
as I do, we may be thankful for your daughter's
escape. The question still remains, who is he?
and how did he become possessed of the knowledge
he has employed for this purpose ?"

They remained silent for some time, each occupied
with his own thoughts. At last Joe said, gravely
and earnestly—

"Ah, Mr. Worsdale, I loved my poor father! I
had never forgotten his indulgence to me, but I was
a spoilt child with the bright world before me. His
death, and the event which happened on the very
date of it, seemed to me in the miserable state in
which I then lay, a judgment of Heaven, and I
vowed, that if I were spared, I would endeavour to
repair my wasted life."

He paused a moment or so. Matthew remained
silent, but he turned round with some expression of
interest in his face; and Dolly, creeping to her
husband's side, took his hand, which trembled a
little, between her own, and said—

"Joe! dear Joe!"

"My darling," Joe said, "I will tell you all now.
I would rather you heard it in your father's
presence. Where I have erred, I have paid the
penalty; and, on the other hand, God has been

graciously pleased to prosper my good resolutions.
You know, Mr. Worsdale, and no one better, after
my poor mother's death, and when your own family
were quite young, how indulged and humoured in
every way I was.   I am afraid you still remember
the airs I gave myself, and the thousand absurdities
I was guilty of.   Ah! they took it out of me at
Harrow, sir! 'Young Devilsdust,' as they called
me!   But when I had learnt to know my place—I
mean the place that every lad can earn who tries to
do so by fair means—and had thrashed a youngster
bigger than myself, who writes his name with a title
before it now, I found the great school then, like
the great world I have seen since, ready and willing
to respect the lad or the man who knows how to
respect himself.   Still, I looked on a life of toil
as so much time snatched from the pleasures of
existence.   I have discovered since, as many of us
do, that labour is not the curse that it is sometimes
painted, but only the heavy shadow, throwing into
strong relief the letters that spell Enjoyment.   My
father's wealth had made me independent of exer-
tion, and I resolved to travel and see the world.
Wealth and inexperience were easy passports to the
pleasures of a continental life, and by the kind
services of a friend I made abroad—an Englishman
—I learnt the mysteries of the gaming table, and
paid the usual tax on knowledge for it.   This man,

accompanied by his wife, a Swiss lady, I believe, and of great personal beauty, lived in the first style. Their pleasant dinner and card parties were perfect. But at last it was whispered that the lady played the part of a confederate, and by some system of signals, previously arranged, she communicated to her husband the contents of his adversary's hand. In the attractiveness of her beauty and address, as well as in her skill, he found a very useful accomplice. I had been induced to play, and had lost heavily, and so invariably, and, as it seemed, strangely, that I began to suspect there was unfairness somewhere. The next day I received a letter from my father, containing his portrait."

" Do you remember the kind of portrait it was ?" Mr. Worsdale asked.

" The last probably he had had taken," Joe answered, " for the hair was white, or nearly so. It was quite a small one, and contained in a locket that could be worn on the watch guard."

" And the letter ?" Matthew added.

" Made a great impression on me," Joe resumed. " It expressed the earnest hope I might one day return to a life of usefulness and industry, in place of the purposeless course I was then pursuing."

" Yes," Matthew said thoughtfully, though more to himself than aloud. " It did so."

"And I remember it spoke of you," Joe continued, "in the strong terms of the manly affection he always entertained for you."

Matthew said nothing, but inclined his head gravely.

"In the hope they might tend to confirm the resolutions I had made, I carried that letter and portrait about with me for some days, and for some little time I was resolute; but one evening the temptation was too strong, and I went to the public table (they were permitted at the place then), and, strange to say, I won nearly every time. Ah! Mr. Worsdale, only those who have played—and won—can understand the fever of the blood and the delirium that success produces! I noticed my English friend was in the room, and observing my success. He joined me when I was leaving, and repeated his invitation to dine with him the following day, rallying me on my good fortune, for we had been somewhat of companions, and I had frankly told him of my father's letter and of my own resolves. This proposal of his I declined, and either my manner, or some word inadvertently dropped by me, gave him a hint of my suspicions, and an altercation ensued. We were in one of the less frequented streets at the time, and as I turned to leave him, a heavy, crushing blow from, I suppose, a loaded stick fell on my head, and I remember nothing further till I found myself lying in a small chamber in a house close by. When I recovered sufficiently to understand what was said to me, I was told that when found lying on the ground unconscious, it was discovered I had been robbed of everything I had had about me, even to my poor father's letter and portrait—a loss that troubled me more than all the rest. I learnt also that a gentleman, a countryman of my own, had paid a trifle for the care the kind people of the house and the surgeon who attended me had shown; but on causing inquiries to be made at the house of my former friend, we learnt he had left the place the day following. I think," Joe continued with a sad smile, " a sick bed in a dirty house, and in a strange town, is a favourable condition for re-flection. Perhaps the terrible blow on the head—I believe the scar may be seen—helped to shake the scales from my eyes, and I saw my purposeless life as it really was. The allurements of play, and the hollow attractions of a dissipated life—laughter without merriment, beauty without truth, the fever of the excitement and the falsehood of the society sickened and palled upon me; and then it was, wearied and disgusted with this world of pleasure, that I remembered more vividly than ever the wishes of my poor father, who, it seems, had died on the very day of the occurrence I refer to, and then I determined to repair, if I could, those few wasted years of my early life."

Here Joe paused.   Matthew said quietly—

" Go on, sir, if you please."

Dolly pressed her husband's hand, and nestling closer to him said—

" Poor Joe !   Poor, dear Joe !"

" Thanks to a good constitution, which had never been unduly tried," Joe continued, " I began soon to recover.   I travelled for a while, endeavouring to restore my health and strength, and to arrange my plans for the future.   The loss of my father's letter weighed heavily on me, and I thought over, many times, the wishes it had expressed.   At last I resolved to make my way to Dalesford, and renew my acquaintance with you, and propose to become a partner in the business, in return for the money I could place in it.   Then I reflected that, with your recollection of my boyhood, your opinion of me might not be very favourable ; and that with sons of your own you might have other views.   But at last I resolved to venture, and rather more than two years ago set out for the purpose."

He paused again, and Matthew said—

" You had better go on, sir ; your solicitor may be here directly."

" I should feel very grieved for you to think worse of me than I deserve," Joe continued, " but I must

ask you to remember that in what I am going to
tell you I felt at the time a soured and disappointed man—disappointed in myself I mean, and
soured by seeing too much of the night-side of
human nature. The men I had known were for the
most part adventurers or fools ; and in the truth
and purity of women, I had but little faith. Well,
with a misgiving how my proposal would be met,
urged on the one side by a reverence for my
father's wish and a desire to do right, and on the
other hand restrained by my own self-distrust and
doubt, I came down to Dalesford here. On the
evening of my arrival I sauntered through the
adjacent country, and came upon a festival or gala
at a place you call Daisy Hill."

He felt the clasp of Dolly's hand tighten on his
own, as, pale and silent, she looked up into his face
with a strange and earnest expression.

" I had been observing the visitors as they passed
me, in loud and vulgar merriment, or with the
affectation of formal and rigid propriety—and had
been thinking, was it strange with such elements to
constitute so much of our middle-class respectability,
that our youth should look elsewhere for the attractions that many of them might fail to find at home,
when I saw a group so different from the rest that
I became strangely interested. We do not observe
etiquette very closely, I think, at such places, or at

all events, I did not, and availing myself of an opportunity to address one of them, I learnt that her 'name was Worsdale, but they called her Dolly at home.' "

" Joe !" Dolly whispered, breathing quickly and blushing deeply.   " Was that you ?—Was it really you ?"

He paused again in his narrative to kiss, in his husband's love and pride, the frank and honest face of the pure-hearted little woman by his side, caressing the gentle head with its long, soft, brown hair falling over her neck and shoulders.

" Then," Joe said, turning to Matthew, " I had a greater fear of your reception of me than before, for I had a greater interest in it ; and then, the doubt and distrust I had acquired of all women, renewed their hold in me (mind, I offer no excuse for this—I am telling you, as far as I can, the simple truth) ; and I thought, Could I but learn the character of this one before the love that, I felt, was springing up in my heart, had gained entire mastery over me ! and in this state of indecision I left Dalesford without presenting myself, and quitted England for Paris, that I might forget the little incident at Daisy Hill.   Well, it might have been the result of the occurrence at the continental town —the nervous depression under which I was suffering ; but my father's letter and my strange meeting with the daughter of his old partner and friend, seemed to me more than a mere coincidence, and at last I decided on the plan I would adopt. I wrote to you from Paris——"

" I remember a letter from Paris, certainly," Matthew said.

" And," Joe continued, " I mentioned a young fellow I was anxious to recommend——"

" I remember that too, of course," the old man said; " perfectly."

" Which young fellow, myself, in due time brought you the letter I had written," Joe said. " That was my deception of you, Matthew Worsdale, but for no unworthy end, as you must know."

" It was one that nearly defeated your purpose," Matthew replied. " The letter written by Mr. Edward Sherwin was no recommendation to me just then, let me tell you !"

" I knew that at our first interview," Joe said, " and I felt I had to face another disappointment ; but I remembered a certain form of words my father had often quoted to me, which had been used to him by a young fellow seeking his fortune many years before."

"Aye?" Matthew said slowly. "Do you remember now what the words were ?"

" ' Look here, master ! ' " Joe said bluntly, " ' I have no money and I have no friends!

can't thieve, and I wont beg—and there you have
it!'"

"Ah!" Matthew said, with a deep breath, and a
softened look coming into his face—"I remember
those words, Joe, very well!"

"My story is nearly done," Joe said. "My term
of service with you, sir, was a happy one. I learnt
to revere and esteem the sterling worth of your own
character, and I felt my love for this dear one
growing more and, more each day.

"In the very place where I had first met her, and
on the anniversary of the very day, I ventured to
declare my love, resolving if it were returned, to tell
you frankly who I was, confess the deception I had
practised, and ask your pardon. You know how
that miserable man who had played the spy and
eavesdropper came between us, how my word was
doubted, and my pride wounded. I felt then most
bitterly the error I had committed in adopting my
device at all, though still I hoped to make it clear
to you at last. Then came the fire——"

"Aye, the fire!" Matthew said, with something
like a groan.

"I know the suspicions you entertained," Joe
said, after a moment's hesitation, "and from one
point of view they did not seem ill-founded. I
think you will scarcely entertain them now?"

"No," Matthew replied slowly and thoughtfully, " scarcely ; but I wish we could learn how it began !"

" We may never be able to do that with certainty," Joe said. " I had locked up the shed Number Four that night, and then all seemed safe. You may remember, at the first outbreak of the fire, we went in there with the engine-hose to try to save the mill ?"

" I remember nothing very distinctly, excepting the calamity itself," Matthew replied sadly.

" Well," Joe answered, " you remember how strict your regulations were, and how every precaution was taken to avoid accidents of that kind ? In shed Number Four, I found this—it may pain you to see it, but in justice to myself, the husband of your daughter, Matthew Worsdale, I show it to you."

He took from his pocket a small meerschaum pipe, with a fantastically carved bowl, and an amber mouthpiece. On a little silver plate on the stem was engraved " Tim Worsdale."

" A few moments more, Mr. Worsdale," Joe continued ; " I will not dwell on our last meeting at your house, except to say I went there with love and forgiveness in my heart, and with the intention of telling you everything. Well, I was prevented. My poor Dolly, my brave little woman !——" Joe added, with a break in his voice, and fondly and proudly pressing his young wife to his bosom, " who left her home, so little understood, my poor darling !—without a word of reproach on her lips, who has never breathed a whisper of resentment since ! who has been so near the grave, that we who knew and loved her already felt the void her leaving us would cause, true to her blessed mission of peace and goodwill, has brought us again together, Matthew Worsdale, and holding her near my heart, I ask you once more can you believe my story, and will you take my hand ?"

Matthew said nothing in reply, but I think his firm old mouth gave way a little, and the lip trembled for a second or so, as he took Joe's right hand within his own and grasped it long and fervently ; and then Dolly knew that the two she loved most in all the world were friends once more, and she had made them so.

CHAPTER VIII.

ONE AND THE SAME MAN.

HEN the servant announced Mr. Titheradge, that gentleman, carrying a professional black leather bag, and looking
watchful and thoughtful as ever, entered the room
with his brisk, but withal soft footstep, and having
shaken hands with Dolly and her husband, was
briefly introduced to Mr. Worsdale. He declined
Joe's invitation to lunch before commencing business, saying, as he took out his large gold watch—

"No, thank you—presently, presently. We are
past our appointed time as it is. I have been in
the house some short time, but heard you were
engaged."

Then, without saying any more, he dipped into the
black bag, and produced some letters, duly docketed,
that had passed between the late Mr. Sherwin and
his son, also a copy of the elder Sherwin's will,
which he said it might be convenient to refer to.
Dolly had withdrawn, and the three being left to
consider the business that had brought them to-

gether, Mr. Titheradge, in a lucid and brief way, stated his client's views (as if Joe himself had not been there) regarding the rebuilding of the mill, and the renewal of the business under the old firm of " Sherwin and Worsdale," to which order of names, though it seemed to give the younger man the precedence, yet as being established by many years, he thought there could be no objection.

Matthew said—

" Certainly not. Go on, if you please."

Mr. Titheradge said, " Quite so;" and after he had selected a few more papers, humming a little tune as he did so, he continued—

" It will be right, Mr. Sherwin, before we go any further, to place Mr. Worsdale in possession of your financial position at the present moment, and then we will submit to him the arrangements you propose."

Joe having duly assented, Mr. Titheradge proceeded to lay before Matthew Worsdale statements that, backed by the evidence of legal and commercial documents, as well as bankers' accounts, satisfied him Joe was in a very much better position in the world than he could have supposed even the son and heir of Job Sherwin would have been ; for beside some excellent investments, which, under the guidance of the shrewd old lawyer, he had made, he had exercised a rigid economy in his affairs, and had had the good fortune besides to make one or two highly successful speculations, which had born negotiated during his sojourn at Dalesford. As he referred to this, Mr. Titheradge added—

"A very remarkable stroke of fortune that was, too !"

"I believe," Joe said fervently, "it was under the influence of the dearest and truest woman in the world! She has been my guardian angel, sir, if ever man had one; for everything has prospered with me that has had a reference to her."

In brief, they decided the factory should be re-built without delay, and the partnership was to be renewed, if not on quite such advantageous terms to Mr. Worsdale—for Mr. Titheradge was a keen adviser in the interests of his client—as he had previously enjoyed, the conditions were sufficiently liberal to promise comfort and competence.

But it would have been contrary to Matthew's character if he had accepted every offer made without some demur or hesitation, and briefly, though cordially acknowledging his obligations, he required time to think over the proposals.

Mr. Titheradge, having hummed a little, suggested a few days—say a week—and then he would be very happy to renew negotiations. This was agreed to, and in consideration of Matthew's journey home, they decided to dine as early as con-

venient. Then Mr. Titheradge put his papers into
his leather bag, which he locked and carried upstairs himself to the room allotted to him for the
night. Mr. Worsdale, having made several memo-
randa in reference to the recent interview, joined
the others in the garden, overlooking the pleasant
dale through which the little stream flowed. Here he
was presented to a comely and bright-eyed matronly
lady, seated on a garden-chair, and holding Dolly's
hand. I think she had been crying a little, for her
eyelashes were wet, and she had just been saying
to Dolly—

"I knew it would all come right, my dear. I
told Titheradge so, when you went away from our
house to the church. If you had been our own
poor Carrie (in 'eaven, my dear), I couldn't have
felt more—and I said———" when Joe approached
them and said—

"Mrs. Titheradge, let me introduce Mr. Worsdale, my wife's father."

The old lady rose, and made her little old-
fashioned half bow, half courtesy, and Matthew
took very quietly the soft plump hand she extended
to him. Dolly told him, in her low and gentle
voice, how kind and good a friend she had found
in her, when she had been ill and thought she was
going to die, at which this foolish old woman let
fall another tear or two, and said—

" Why, my own dear, nothing could be too good
for you, I'm sure !"

And then Matthew, stretching out his broad,
strong palm, and taking the old lady's hand between his own, pressing it warmly as he did so,
said, as he slightly inclined his head in his own
sturdy way—

" I thank you, ma'am. I can only thank you ;
but may God Almighty bless you !"

They had a very pleasant dinner, and a very
good one. There was a certain rich gravy soup,
that Dolly herself had prepared that morning, that
was a great success. I do not suppose it occurred
to her father that it was her womanly thought of
him that had reminded her to make his favourite
dish ; but he ate of it heartily—and more than
once—to the evident pleasure of the bright little
mistress of the house that presided so pleasantly at
the table. Mr. Titheradge, as I hope we know,
was no longer a man of business at dinner, and his
genial politeness of that old school in which he had
been a student, was to the reciprocal advantage of
his own and the simple, frank manner of Joe, as
well as the sturdy bearing of old Matthew.

It was later in the evening, and they were
seated over the coffee in the drawing-room. The
conversation had become general, and among other
subjects the rapid growth of Dalesford, and the

development of the trade that now formed its staple, had been referred to.

" By the way," said Mr. Titheradge, " I have the son of one of your townsmen in my chambers, who is seeing London practice—Mr. Ossett."

" And a very charming young man, my dear," his lady remarked to Dolly. " I suppose you would know him."

" Only slightly," Dolly said ; " but," she added, " she had heard him highly spoken of."

" And it was rather strange he should have been dining at our house one day, when you were getting better and had been out for a drive with Mr. Sherwin."

Joe exchanged glances with Mr. Titheradge, and said—

" Frank Ossett is a good fellow ! I believe a better fellow does not live !"

" Why, Joe," Dolly said, " when did you become acquainted ?"

Her husband smiled as the scene of the Hallelujah Band recurred to him, and answered—

" Our first meeting was a strange one enough, and our last—" he became grave here, as he remembered how in that interview he had fathomed the poor lad's secret of his love for Dolly. " Well, he's an honest, true young fellow," he resumed, " and a gentleman."

Mrs. Titheradge, on whom Frank's manly and withal modest address had made the impression that such qualities usually produce on a sound-hearted woman, was at once loud in her praises of the young fellow ; to all of which Mr. Titheradge said—

"Oh, quite so—quite so !"

But Matthew Worsdale sat silent. It might be that other matters occupied his thoughts, or that he involuntarily fell to comparing in his own mind the character of his son's early companion and friend, with that of the worthless lad who was acquiring experience of life in barracks. But they took little notice of the old man, perhaps for reasons of their own, and left him to himself.

"Were you intimate with Mr. Ossett?" Mrs. Titheradge asked.

"Not exactly intimate," Joe answered. "On the occasion I refer to, I had been dining with him. We were having a pleasant evening, and were chatting about Dalesford, when a friend of his came in—a gentleman in the army, if I recollect aright. His appearance struck me ; and I remember that better than I do his name. He had the rather unusual combination we sometimes meet with in persons who have lived in hot and moist climates—white hair and a dark moustache."

There was a sudden pause in the conversation at this; Joe seeming quite unconscious of the surprise he had caused. Even Matthew turned round on his chair, and looked steadily at him.

" Had you seen him before, do you think ?" Mr. Titheradge inquired, and began to hum a little.

" Well," Joe said, looking before him with half-closed eyes, as if trying to recollect, " I cannot quite say. There was an indefinable something in his eyes and his voice that had some vague association with it ; but I cannot tell what it was. I don't set much store by the impression I had. It was very likely a caprice of my own fancy. I remember when I was in Dalesford, on the evening of the Christmas gathering at the mill, being over-taken by a man in a cloak, who wore his hair long, and had a sort of Spanish hat pulled over his face ; he asked some unimportant questions—I forget what—but left the same vague feeling on my mind that I describe."

" Perhaps those persons with the appearance you mention," Mr. Titheradge said, quietly—" I mean those with the white hair and dark moustache—are more common than you suppose. A gentle-man with the same peculiarity waited on me eighteen months ago, and made inquiries concerning you. I had no information I could give; and after a short interview, he left."

"What did he say his name was?" Matthew asked, shortly.

"Well, at this moment," the lawyer said, "I really cannot say. He was a military-looking man, I recollect, and I made a note of his name and business in my diary, but it was so unimportant I had almost forgotten it. Probably some one you had known abroad?" he added, turning to Joe.

"I knew no one with that appearance, certainly," Joe replied.

"Did he say his name was Captain Clarence?" Dolly asked.

"That wasn't the name he gave," Mr. Titheradge replied. "It was a Colonel—something—but I can easily ascertain on my return."

"I always thought it strange," Dolly said, "that the Captain Clarence whom my sister and Miss Skimple, our governess, knew at Redwell, should introduce himself to our house as Mr. Edward Sherwin."

"It was stranger still," Matthew said, slowly, "that he should have with him a portrait of Mr. Sherwin's father."

"Of my father!" Joe said.

"Yes," Matthew continued; "and the letter—

in the well-known handwriting—the last he ever wrote to his son when abroad."

"I remember the portrait," Dolly said, "and our comparing it with one we had, and which he had not recognised."

"Why, that letter and the portrait," Joe exclaimed, "must surely have been the same that I lost that night!"

In reply to some questions of Mr. Titheradge, Joe repeated briefly that episode in his life, which comprised the meeting in the gaming-house, and the subsequent assault and robbery.

"That seems to me," Mr. Titheradge said, quietly, "to furnish a clue to the affair. In all probability it was your English friend who robbed you while you lay unconscious on the ground, and took, besides your money, the letter and the miniature, which he afterwards employed as evidence to support his assumed character; and it is my theory that the military gentleman who inquired after you at my chambers—the Captain Clarence your wife refers to—the gentleman who introduced himself at Dalesford as Mr. Sherwin, junior—the scoundrel who robbed you, and perhaps the mysterious person in the hat and cloak, are simply one and the same man."

CHAPTER IX.

NEMESIS.

OW it happened that the letter addressed by Messrs. Titheradge and Burnley to Mr. Worsdale, and which lay at the bottom of all the events recorded in the previous chapter, had travelled (presumably at least, being delivered on the same day) in the same post-bag to Manchester with one to Lady Petitoe, written in that bold back-handed style that many persons, women as well as men, adopt, who have much manuscript labour to get through. It is not therefore to be wondered at that Dr. Rachel Gambado, who held a diploma from the medical college of Bunkumville (Mass.), the author (not "authoress," you are requested to take note) of "Pathological Pastimes," "Convictions of a Clinical Convert," and "A Popular Inquiry into the Primary Causes of Scorbutic Eruptions," among other masculine attributes, professed a style of caligraphy striking and original. Indeed, it would have been difficult to guess the kind of pen she preferred for the purpose; whether it had been constructed from the pinion of an ostrich, or converted from the reed of a Pandean pipe; or with a view to the economy of time, was identical with one of her own fingers. When John took the letter in, he remarked to Mary, who was sweeping out the hall passage, that the chap who had wrote that there must have been blessed with a wooden leg, and had utilised it for the purposes of correspondence. Mary had surmised he must be a beauty, whoever he was; and Cook wondered they didn't charge extra postage. If they could have known what that large superscription portended—if they could have guessed the kind of visitor whose coming that letter announced, their remarks might have been more damaging, perhaps even libellous. In a brief, manly strain, it informed the astonished Lady Petitoe and the slightly startled Skimple, that before she left Liverpool for New York, Dr. Rachel Gambado proposed to take Manchester in her way, as she desired to increase her acquaintance with that important manufacturing centre and its large operative population, with a view to her projected work, "Life and the Loom, a Critical Inquiry into the Average of Existence."

Our dear Skimple was not pleased by the proposal. I do not hesitate to say she admired Dr. Rachel Gambado and Miss Whyte Grannit and

Mr. Pompey Wampum greatly; but it was the admiration she felt for the Pyramids of Egypt, or the Winged Bulls of Nineveh—in their proper places and at a convenient distance—but she did not care to contemplate them on the hearth-rug of domestic life. I believe a request, however politely preferred, for temporary house-room for the Colossus of Rhodes, or the selection of the front garden as a site for Cleopatra's Needle or Pompey's Pillar, would not have been more unwelcome than the prospect of the Medical Professor of Bunkumville (Mass.), taking up her residence, though for a short time only, in that cosy and exclusive Broughton villa.

Miss Skimple's manifest discomfiture unsettled also her nervous ladyship, who proposed at once to put the house into brown holland and paper, and flee away to the nearest watering-place. But it was too late. The stupendous Intellect with the Strident Voice arrived next day, and when it walked up to the front door in a large hat (called familiarly, I believe, a "flop") and short skirts, and wearing what looked very like Wellington boots, Broughton confessed it had never seen such a sight before. The cabman, who had erroneously estimated his own acumen as opposed to the Doctor's decisive action, when he endeavoured to extract an illegal sixpence, felt his anger evaporate rapidly by

the contemplation of the Doctor's figure seen rear-
wards. His annoyance was transmuted into playful
sarcasm, for he inquired of Mary whether there
was going to be a fair in those parts, and the
probable charge per head for admission at feeding-
time; and he reminded John he had caught a
good 'un this time, and would he mind telling him
what bait he used? The amazement the Doctor
created did not end there. When she walked up
the stairs, two or three steps at a time, Cook surmised it was a burglar in disguise, whose intention
was to murder them all in their sleep, and to rob
the house before the morning.

Altogether, the domestics of that villa had not
had such a merry time for many a day. John's
roguish expressions in reference to Wellington
boots, Cook's imitation of the voice and gait, and
Mary's description of her manners in the parlour,
and the way she kissed Poker (under which figure
of speech she was understood to refer to the companion of Lady Petitoe, even our Skimple), aroused
their hilariousness to such an extent that more
than once Miss Skimple was constrained, in the
interests of that respectability in which she so
fervently believed, to inquire what such unseemly
conduct meant. It was of no use. The entire
household was revolutionised in less than an hour.
The authoritative manner with which Dr. Gambado

insisted on feeling Lady Petitoe's pulse, the arbitrary tone she assumed when she bade her put out her tongue, and the deliberate, not to say heartless, way in which she wrote out a prescription, in that wonderful handwriting, on a sheet of letter paper, with genuine apothecary's cypher, might well have shaken the strongest nerves. She irritated the housemaid by pulling the bag out of the chimney in her bedroom, and early the next morning walked up and down the garden path, with her hands locked behind her, and in a dress I am afraid to describe. Under these difficulties Miss Skimple fell back on her good-breeding, and Lady Petitoe fell back on her well-bred friend. No comment had been passed by either; but when her ladyship had been strengthened by a glass of sherry at luncheon, she ventured to ask Miss Simple—

" Do you think, dear, she will stay long ?"

With that knowledge of her sex, or some of them, with which we must credit that sagacious person, Miss Skimple replied—

" As long, my dear, I have no doubt, as it suits her convenience."

And it soon became apparent that Dr. Rachel Gambado's convenience was a point of great importance in Dr. Rachel's opinion. In her hard and loud voice she inquired what Lady Petitoe's views were for the occupation of the day. And her ladyship, who had very few views of her own, timidly referred to her friend. But before Miss Skimple could reply, the Doctor stated her own intentions very plainly.

"Because," said she, " as I hev a few calls to make, I should feel obleeged if you could loan me your chariot ; and as there would be room for tew, p'raps you'd be glad to accompany me ?"

Lady Petitoe looked appealingly to her companion, who seemed desirous, for some reason of her own, to preserve as much distance as was practicable between her patroness and their visitor ; and she replied with that simple sincerity which is so delightful a quality in well-educated persons of the Skimple school, that she should feel charmed.

Nothing but her implicit faith in Miss Skimple could have reconciled her nervous ladyship to the trial of seeing her neatly-appointed brougham in the temporary possession of their energetic guest ; and even then, after their departure, her depression was so great that she was found by the housemaid among the remains of the luncheon, bathed in tears, and refusing to be comforted.

The Doctor was prepared with quite a bundle of letters of introduction, and these she read over to herself in the carriage, leaving Miss Skimple to her own reflections. Some of the millowners on whom she called received her with but scant courtesy, evidently begrudging the valuable time, which, as business men, they were asked to bestow on an inquisitive stranger; others answered the Doctor's questions civilly, but briefly; while others again, such as foremen or junior partners of the firm, declined, unless authorised by their superiors or seniors, to admit her to view the works; possibly with an impression she was there under false pretences, striving to obtain some hint which might be to the injury of their own branch of trade. However, it was all one to the Doctor; she asked her questions and made her notes. The rebuffs she encountered were to her energetic and persistent nature as the small shot that rattles against and falls flattened from the skin of the rhinoceros; and the satirical remarks on her dress and personal appearance completely failed, as far as she herself was concerned. But it was different in the case of Miss Skimple. She was painfully conscious of the slightly irregular costume of her learned friend, and the small shafts of ridicule that glanced hurtless from the impervious bark that shielded the sturdy nature of the Doctor, were by no means without their effect on the more susceptible character of her highly respectable companion.

We have it on record that a certain arrow, many years ago, struck against a tree in the New Forest (said to be an oak, but I am of opinion it

12—2

was an American pine, or hemlock, or some Trans-
atlantic shrub), and glancing from that invulnerable
trunk, fatally wounded a Royal personage, who unfortunately happened to be in the vicinity. Thus
it was, after a personal remark reflecting on the
Doctor's choice of a hatter and bootmaker, that Miss
Skimple, on whom the bolt fell, with a martyr-like
expression of countenance, ventured to inquire—

"Have you done now, dear ?"

"Done !" the Doctor replied, in a voice of
thunder, as she took her seat in the brougham.
"We have seen, briefly it is true, but sufficient for
our purpose, the ' Life at the Loom ;' let us now
seek to investigate the ' Life in the Home.'
Stop !" she shouted to the coachman. "That will
do ! I want to get down here."

They were being driven through a miserable
street in the worst part of the outlying town, and
the carriage was drawn up at the end of a noisome
alley. Now, whatever our Skimple's compassion
might be for the suffering wretches who are poor,
she had certainly an equal amount of sympathy for
those other suffering wretches who, pleasantly
fixed in the world, surrounded by comforts and
competence, are yet fated to be immolated on the
altar of social propriety or self-interest. This was
her case at the present ; but she could not consent,
victim as she felt herself to be, voluntarily to

submit to a further martyrdom. So she discreetly elected to remain in the brougham, while her more vigorous companion pursued her inquiries in the dirty and offensive alley or yard known as Miller's Rents.

A churlish ruffian boy, with a shoeblack's block beside him, was lying on the dirty flagstone outside one of the miserable tenements, trying to pick out a tune on a tin whistle. Dr. Rachel rapped his shock head with her hard knuckles, and asked in her stern voice—

" Who lives here ?"

He looked at her for a moment, and an expression of cunning crept into his small dull eyes as he said—

" Me."

" Have you any parents, boy ?" the Doctor demanded.

" What on 'em ?" the boy answered.

" I want to see your father," the Doctor said, shortly.

" Do yer ?" the boy asked. " Oh, ah. Now then."

And removing his tin whistle from his mouth, he uttered instead a few notes by means of his little finger placed crookwise between his lips.

A woman appeared in the doorway at the moment, standing in such an attitude that she

effectually barred any ingress on the part of
Doctor Rachel, and even prevented her seeing
inside the room.

"Now, then, what was yer wanting?" she
asked, in a coarse, rough voice.

Dr. Rachel Gambado looked at the woman with
interest—a type of the operative family, as she
inferred, to be fully described and commented on in
her projected work. She looked at her, as the
woman stood there, ragged and dirty, a wisp of
coarse hair twisted into a hard nob at the back of
her head, and with a mark or two on her wasted
face that were neither set there by nature, nor
looked like the results of an accident.

" Hev yew a husband, my good woman?" Dr.
Rachel asked.

" What's that do wi' you?" the woman answered.

" Yew can answer or not, as yew please," the
Doctor resumed; " but I hev my reasons for
asking. I want to know, hev yew a husband? If so,
where is he to be found?—(the door of a cupboard
in the room moved slightly, and the woman stood
more firmly in the doorway than before). Is he
at work? If so, what? What are his wages
weekly? Air yew married to him? Hev yew any
fam'ly? What are they, an' how many? An' what
may be yewer weekly expenditoor?"

" I do'ant know what you're wanting," the

woman said, roughly; "but I ain't got no mester, theer! He ain't got no work to do if I had; an' he wouldn't do any work if he had it to do, theer! An' do you mind your own business, and we'll mind ourn—theer, then!"

Finding she could obtain no information, Dr. Rachel Gambado made a note of the same, and withdrew from the court, followed by the loud and virulent abuse of the woman, and the coarse jests and jeers of the ruffian boy, and such of his companions as had been attracted by the Doctor's strange appearance.

As she re-entered the brougham, Mr. Stepper came forth from the closet. He seated himself on the remains of a chair, drew a long breath, and wiping his white lips with the sleeve of his coat, said, with a ghastly smile—

"I thought I wur spotted! Shiner, fetch us a sup o' beer."

"Shall I tell John to drive home, dear?" Miss Skimple inquired.

"No," the Doctor returned, shortly. "Most unsatisfactory. But it is some reward for one's labours, however barren they may appear, to enj'y the anticipation of a favourite indulgence. Drive to the hospital."

"The hospital!" Miss Skimple cried.

"The hospital," Dr. Rachel answered. "I hev

a letter tew the resident surgeon, as well as tew the visiting faculty, and nothing could indoose me tew forego the pleasure of a visit."

Now as there are many good people in the world, who, disclaiming all feelings of superstition, can never be, notwithstanding, induced to pass underneath a ladder, or commence an undertaking on a Friday, or walk through a churchyard after dark, so we may meet with others who have an unconquerable antipathy to the vicinity of an infirmary, as if contagion stood like a hall-porter in the doorway, and infection ascended with the smoke from the chimneys.   And such was Miss Skimple, but it was in vain that she endeavoured to excuse herself.   Dr. Rachel Gambado felt she would be on her own ground there, and would take no denial. She, the advocate of her sex's right to challenge competition with the lords of the creation in the noble art of surgery, one of the acknowledged champions of the movement that was to secure to that sex its proper position in the world, was only too proud of an occasion when she could practically illustrate the benefit of that training, that had gained her the proud distinction of a diploma from the medical college of Bunkumville.   Our Skimple, we know, was a strong-minded person, but her power lay rather in wily influence than assertive force, and she would gladly have shrunk from the proposed visit. But, as in the history of that once honoured British institution, now defunct, the P.R., we may meet with many instances of science and strategy having to succumb to the fierce onslaught of vigour and impetuosity, so was the sagacious Skimple but an infant in the massive grasp of the Gambado. She had no longer any power to decline, and although the Doctor's vivid descriptions of difficult operations and critical cases somewhat unsettled her nervous stamina, Miss Skimple yielded to inevitable fate, and in a few minutes found herself being presented to the resident surgeon of the hos‧ pital, as a member of that " popular and ever- growing movement, which was to place within Woman's hand the mysteries of the curative art and of operative science, and which was, at no dis‧ tant period, tew ennoble," &c.

If Dr. Rachel had been self-possessed in her interviews with the brusque foremen and junior partners of the factories, and impassive under the virulence of the sorely tried and degraded woman of Miller's Rents, her bearing here was simply beyond all admiration. Her perfect mastery of the technicalities, her thorough familiarity with all the details, and the acute interest she displayed, were so remarkable, that the amazed Skimple remained speechless. I am not sure that, more than once, a faint suggestion of a womanly blush did not struggle to the Skimple cheek, and perhaps a slight sensation of feminine shame tingled near the roots of the few remaining grey hairs under that smooth brown front, but they were not shared by her companion. I suppose that all such weaknesses had long since been suppressed by the prompt scientific treatment of the Bunkumville College.

The two ladies had made the round of the hospital, with a female nurse in attendance, and Dr. Rachel had made copious notes, and asked a multitude of questions, and Miss Skimple's hopes of speedily returning home began to revive, when the Doctor said suddenly—

" Now, then, hev yew a casualty ward—say ?"

" My dear," Miss Skimple said, " had we not better defer——"

But the Doctor bestowed scarcely a look on her, and, accompanying the nurse, desired her to follow. The casualty ward was not full, but there was quite enough to shock and pain the on-looker. It had no effect, however, on the Doctor. She walked from bedside to bedside, and the poor suffering inmates turned a dull and inquiring eye as the strange figure moved past. Feeling sick and somewhat ashamed, Miss Skimple slowly followed. She had paused at the bed-foot of a little boy, who had met with some accident in the crowded street. She was looking at the poor little pale face in the repose of his child's sleep, and was wondering what his thoughts would be, when he first realised the loss he had been compelled to suffer, but she was roused by the loud tones of the Doctor, saying—

" Yes, very interesting case indeed ! Miss Skimple, step this way; yew will be lifted considerable by this subject. I guess he will hev to be trephined. Garrotted, was he ? Oh—an' brought in by the police on duty—ah ——''

But even the Doctor looked surprised for a moment at the dismay that was depicted on Miss Skimple's white face. She had caught hold of a chair, and was leaning against the wall for support, gazing intently and speechless at the patient on the bed; for with features rigid, the white hair still stained with the blood that had flowed from the savage blow, and the dark moustache, in strong contrast to the deathly hue of the skin, lay the man she had known as Captain Clarence, in whose presence she had always felt that unaccountable agitation, and whom she had so recently seen in the vigour of life and health.

As superior women, like Dr. Rachel Gambado, have but little time, and as little inclination, for indulgence in sentiment, and relegate such amiable weaknesses to their more feminine sisterhood, who have been either denied by nature their own masculine attributes, or whose probationary term as social reformers, or advanced spirits, has been too brief for the extinguishment of all womanly tenderness, the Bunkumville professor was soon engaged again in the inspection of the hospital, leaving her companion, with the attendant of the ward, at the bedside of the wounded man. He was in that sad state of semi-consciousness when the unrestrained thoughts run wild, rousing up memories of the long-buried past, and when the words ramble forth, at times incoherently, and again with a strange link of meaning and of sequence. But this had no interest for the Doctor. It is proverbial how time flies when pleasantly employed, and what with the examination of the operating-room, conversation with the attendant nurse, and discussions with some of the resident authorities, it was close upon an hour when the eminent American took her seat in the brougham. Even then she was not aware apparently of her companion's absence, so engrossed was she in the purpose of her visit; and it was not until she aroused the coachman, who was enjoying a placid nap on the box, and desired him to drive home, that John's inquiry for Miss Skimple recalled that lady's existence to her recollection.

The truly active mind is never at a loss for a resource; and producing her note-book, Dr. Rachel was soon deeply engaged in its contents, and she took little notice of her companion's prolonged absence. At last, as she was closing her book, Miss Skimple appeared at the door of the hospital, and slowly and with apparent difficulty she was making her way to the carriage. Perhaps a less eminent person than the Doctor, or one less occupied with the importance of her own errand in life, and with more sympathy for others, might have observed the evident distress and anguish of mind that the poor lady appeared to be enduring. With a dazed look on her white face and a trembling hand, she was endeavouring to open the door of the carriage.

At that moment, a small boy with a round, merry face and bright eyes, advanced and said, blithely—

" Allow me, ma'am !"

" Oh, thank you, little boy," Miss Skimple said, as the lad held the door open for her.

" Little boy !" said the lad, grinning. " Philip Worsdale, Esquire, if you please, Miss Skimple. I hope you are well, ma'am ?"

" Philip Worsdale !" Miss Skimple exclaimed, turning round as she was about to enter the carriage, and regarding him intently. " So it is. Good Heaven ! This is surely providential ! Tell your father, Philip Worsdale," she continued with difficulty, but clearly and firmly, " and your sister, that the man they called Edward Sherwin is now lying dead in the accident ward of the hospital."

She said but little during the drive homewards, and that in a low and constrained tone, as if she were striving to control a strong emotion. Arrived at home she entered the house silently, and at once retired to her own chamber.

When some time afterwards Lady Petitoe, surprised at her long absence, went herself in search of her, she found her seated in her dress as she had left the carriage—pale and abstracted, gazing wistfully at a miniature she held between her hands, with the tears of some awakened memory rolling down her sorrow-stricken face.

" My dear! oh, my dear! whatever is it ?" Lady Petitoe anxiously asked, for her friend's unwonted emotion affected herself.

" He knew me !" Miss Skimple said, in a hoarse and broken voice, and speaking more to herself than her friend. " Praise be to God, who has brought us together once more! He knew me!— Yes, we knew each other at last !"

" Who?—what is it, my dear?" her friend asked again.

" He had been wandering in his mind," Miss Skimple said, as if still speaking to herself; " and he called me by my name—the name he used to call me by in the old, old days! Ah me! ah me!" the poor woman cried, in a burst of uncontrollable grief. " I knew all then! I knew why his voice

had always so disturbed me! But oh, so changed
—so changed from this!" she cried, gazing on the
little portrait while her tears fell fast. " But when
I pushed his hair back and saw the scar I remembered so well, then I knew him again! and, hoping
and fearing, I called him by his name; and he
seemed to remember everything, for he raised himself on his bed, and looked as he used to look in
the years gone by! Those years—when we were
young, and I, at least, was happy!"

She paused here, and placing her handkerchief
to her eyes swayed herself to and fro, moaning in a
low voice in the bitter anguish of her recollection.
Lady Petitoe, bewildered by this strange manifesta-
tion of poignant grief in one usually so self-
contained, remained silent for a few moments, and
then sought to arouse her by softly laying her
hand on Miss Skimple's shoulder, and saying
gently—

" What is all this, my dear? Wont you tell
me ?"

" He took my hand then," the poor lady said ;
" he bent his head over it, and said something I
could not quite hear; but I knew what he meant.
And I said, ' Yes—everything! everything! as I
hope myself to be forgiven!' And I said the
prayers that came first into my thoughts, and when
I looked again, he was—Dead !"

" Dead !" the other repeated.

" Dead !" Miss Skimple said, with a somewhat
firmer voice, though she spoke in short and broken
sentences.   " But I know he died penitent.
Thank God for His many mercies !—he has died
penitent !"   She took the little portrait, and gazed
at it tenderly.   " This was his face as I knew it
first !   He is at rest now—at rest now, and the
fierce and wicked passions are no more—his sins
repented !   Ah! what am I, poor weak, erring
mortal that I am ! to say I cannot forget my
wrongs ?   Oh !" she continued, seeming unconscious of the other's presence, bowing her head
reverently, and raising her hands in the attitude of
prayer, " Forgive us all our trespasses, as we forgive
those that trespass against us !   Thy will be done,
dear Lord—Thy will be done !"

For you will please to observe—I have no doubt
you have already done so in your journey through
life—that a distinction is to be made between the
people who are heartless and those who are hard-
hearted.   The first are born in the fortunate
possession of an organ that discharges all its func-
tions with vigour and regularity; the auricles and
ventricles, veins and arteries, are all in perfect
working order, and being utterly devoid of those
attributes which sentimental persons associate with
that vital part—such as love, honour, tenderness,

or sympathy, it frequently attains, in an undisturbed and placid series of pulsations, to a very advanced old age, and then at last becomes dead to itself, as it has been dead to others from the beginning. But there is another character we sometimes confound with it, which, if we could only examine carefully, we should find has become hardened and weather-stained by exposure to the storms and trials of life, and which, in spite of its cold and guarded manner, will sometimes by mere accident—nay, even by its own warm, though hidden impulses—burst through the hard and frozen surface, like the strange springs of Iceland, that bubble up vigorous and hot in the midst of the gloom and rigour of a northern winter.

And so this poor, wronged, world-hardened old woman, with the pure, simple Christian faith and hope of her girl-nature coming back fresh upon her, in the tender recollection of her one love, forgave her enemy, and prayed for one that had so despitefully used and persecuted her.

CHAPTER X.

TIME AND TIDE.

IT was quite five years before I again visited Dalesford. The small though busy town I had previously known, had expanded considerably during that time. The stile whereon Mr. Thomas Stepper had rested, when revolving his schemes for defrauding Tim Worsdale; and the footpath, along which the Reverend Ernest Palethorpe had hastened, excited and embarrassed, when he unfortunately took his way to Daisy Hill on the evening so memorable to Dolly and her lover, were either destroyed or obscured by the erection of buildings, or the laying out of new streets and roadways It is interesting, but somewhat saddening, to traverse these upstart towns, which a new branch of industry or rapidly extending trade has created or enlarged, and to observe how glimpses of the former country associations may be traced in some old-fashioned turnstile, or disused well, with its wheel and axle slowly rotting before the onward march of progress and improve-

ment. The names retained by some of the streets
and thoroughfares suggest a rusticity strangely
at variance with their present surroundings; and
" Bluebell Row," " Meadow Side," " Orchard
Place," and " Lovers' Walk," denote very frequently dirty corners, squalid houses, noisome
alleys, and sometimes fever-tainted lanes and
yards, where wild flowers have been strangers for
many a year, and where any odour suggesting the
pleasant perfume of field or garden could not be
recognised by the most imaginative visitor.

But Dalesford was a thriving place, and the
local trade was at its best. The large new mill of
" Sherwin and Worsdale" had been completed
about three years, and had given work to many
scores of willing hands. Naturally enough, there
had been a good deal of talk on the subject of the
unlooked-for return of the younger Sherwin, and
his subsequent marriage with Mr. Worsdale's
daughter; but as we have seen, I think, how Joe
Boothroyd had kept his own counsels, and how
little Mr. Worsdale was given to talking of his
private affairs, many failed to recognise under his
altered appearance and improved circumstances the
former foreman of the mill, or perhaps did not
care to pursue inquiries that received only a caustic,
if a quiet response. We may be sure that Mr.
Sherwin could afford to be independent of his

townsmen's opinion, and might even keep himself aloof, if he chose, when we remember that in addition to his wealth his trade was not a merely local one; and so the good people of Dalesford were soon satisfied to treat with civility and respect the man who always paid promptly, subscribed liberally for charitable and worthy objects, and did good in his own quiet way.

I believe the Reverend Ernest Palethorpe, before he married and left Dalesford to accept a curacy in Kent, had had his suspicions, and did not hesitate to whisper them; though when subsequently introduced to Mr. Sherwin, who had now a bearded face and was in such different attire, his faith was shaken in the identity he had suspected. Indeed Mrs. Batley, who had formerly twitted the curate with his partiality for Mr. Worsdale's daughter, told him bluntly that his suspicions were only the result of an unchristian envy on his part, because a finer fellow than he had carried off his favourite lady. The curate had blushed deeply, and thought the remark "uncalled for;" but he was silent for the remainder of the evening. Certainly some of the good people who were of a lively or an inquisitive turn, complained in their own circle of the pride that always accompanies stuck-up nobodies, and remarked it was the duty of all true Christians, who had been blessed by Providence with enough and to spare of this world's goods, to circulate their money, and disseminate brotherly love by social gatherings in the form of dinners or evening assemblies, and to which they themselves would, of course, expect to be invited, or would have been outrageously offended if passed over.

But there were two or three who had enjoyed the liberal hospitality of Mr. Sherwin's house, and they spoke freely and warmly of it. They could tell how there was generally a visitor, perhaps more, staying in the house, though not Dalesford people certainly, and what good company they were. During one autumn an artist had been frequently noticed sketching in the neighbourhood, who, when his morning's work was done, used invariably to be seen wending his way to the Lodge. On another occasion, a visitor at the house had accompanied the master to the mill, and displayed much interest in the works; and, in consequence of a somewhat unusual personal appearance, had been set down as a foreigner of distinction, though I believe he was only an old "Bohemian" friend of Edward Sherwin, that had settled down as an industrious journalist, and was then engaged in contributing a series of papers on our national manufactures to the pages of a popular magazine.

Mr. Frank Ossett declared Rosedale was the

most charming place he had ever visited, as well
as the brightest and the jolliest, for he had spent a
Christmas there, and was well qualified to judge.
And as for Doll—he meant Mrs. Sherwin—she
looked—by Jove, sir! better than ever.

For this young fellow (who, as I heard, had had
a narrow escape from being turned back in his
examination, while the ungainly Rawley Todd had
passed easily, as a matter of course) had, on the
death of his father, been admitted into the firm of
Titheradge and Burnley as the youngest partner—
though I don't know on what terms with that
keen, but kindly practitioner—and came to Dalesford
only occasionally now; and at such times he had
a standing invitation to make Rosedale his home.
But Mr. Frank had availed himself of it on one or
two occasions only, and used to patronise the
"Talbot" instead.

I believe, myself, he had not got over his love
for the girl who was now another man's wife, and
that he knew it; and that he thought in his own
manly and simple heart he was acting more like a
true gentleman in abstaining from visiting at her
house.

These good and simple fellows are still to be found,
with something in their characters of the chivalry
of other days, that has outlived the many changes
of time. A sense of honour, and a love of fair

play and right dealing, that is inborn, and has no reference whatever to Norman origin, blue blood, or a genealogical tree.   If our records have been truly written, cases may be quoted where our most cherished and honoured guest has been the first to betray our confidence.   Even the minister who has read for our benefit the blessed Sermon on the Mount; or the medical adviser, whom we trusted as a counsellor, or confided in as a friend, has abused the advantage his profession conferred. And it is a comfort to turn to these true hearts, that our wounded faith in human nature may be healed again.   And such was Frank Ossett, and such his friend " Joe" knew him to be.

" You have got your dear mother's beautiful eyes, little Dolly !" Frank had said, as he took Mr. Sherwin's little daughter on his knee, and smoothed the soft brown hair from the bright face ; '' and you must grow up like her, my dear, and be a blessing to all who know you, and a gleam of sunlight and a comfort to everybody, as she has been, little Dolly, and God bless her for it !"

" My name isn't Dolly," the little one had said, speaking as well as she could, and looking with a surprised expression at her new friend's thoughtful face ; " my name is Nelly Sherwin, and I am three years old."

"Ah, you shall be 'Dolly' to me, and no other name, my little one!" Frank had said; and so he called her ever afterwards; and I think it quite possible that in every word of kindness addressed to Nelly, he was uttering the love he had so long and honourably felt for the little one's mother.

It was at breakfast time, during a visit of Frank's to Rosedale Lodge, that Mr. Sherwin opened one of a little heap of letters by that morning's post, and having paused and read it again, said to his wife, with the twinkle in the eyes that we have remarked occasionally in Joe Boothroyd—

"Here is a letter, Dolly, that refers to a friend of yours.   You will be interested, I am sure."

"Of mine, Joe?" Dolly asked; for to the last she called her husband by the name under which she had first known him.   "Who is it?"

"Stay, though," Mr. Sherwin said, turning to Frank; "he is a gentleman for whom you had a great partiality.   I'll read it aloud; it will interest you both :—

"The Rectory, Heron's Mount,
"June — 18—.

"MY DEAR SIR,—My pleasant associations of Dalesford, the scene of my earliest labours and triumphs, and the very delightful relations I enjoyed with Mr. Worsdale's estimable family, are sources of ever-recurring pleasurable reminiscences, and I need scarcely say with what sincere gratification I learnt the alliance of yourself with the charming daughter of that worthy man. My dearest wife, whose health has suffered from over-taxed energies in promoting education among the poor of my parish, desires her best love to Mrs. Sherwin and your dear little pets——"

(" Joe !" Dolly interrupted, " who is it ?")

" And hopes she has not quite forgotten her sweet sister's early and attached friend, ' little Pattie,' fervently trusting to renew, at no distant period, a friendship she has ever cherished among her most precious memories."

(" But I never knew any one of that name, Joe," Mrs. Sherwin replied.)

(" My dear," Joe said, " the writer adopts that strain at the commencement of his letter, as hospitable persons propose a tonic before dinner, that we may digest more favourably what is to follow. Let me proceed.")

" I have no doubt you have learnt, ere this, that in compliance with a very numerously signed requisition, from the most influential persons in the neighbourhood, the Bishop of the diocese has been pleased to appoint me to this living, rendered vacant recently by the lamented demise of the late Rector ; and the parishioners, in accordance with a suggestion thrown out by a highly-valued fellow-

labourer in the vineyard, have requested my ac-
ceptance of a most munificent subscription list,
with a view to the erection of a more suitable
building in the place of the present small and in-
commodious Rectory. Large and unexpected as
this liberality has been, I am informed the sum
subscribed is at least £200 beneath the lowest estimate that has been delivered, and in conformity
with the wish of the parish, and the other very
numerous subscribers, it has been determined to
meet the deficiency, if possible, by appealing to
those Christian friends on whose help and succour
we may rely. Pray accept our united warmest
regards, and if you should desire to assist the
object my esteemed parishioners have so much at
heart, you may—as it may tend to save time and
trouble—forward at once a cheque to—

"Yours, very sincerely,

"My dear Sir,

"In Spirit and in Truth,

"ERNEST PALETHORPE."

"What!" Mrs. Dorothy Sherwin cried, flushing
crimson; "that wicked, slandering Ernest Palethorpe! Why, Joe dear, you can't mean it!"

"How much shall I send, Dolly?" Joe asked,
quietly.

"Send!" Dolly exclaimed. "Send to him! I

wonder how he dare write a begging letter to you, of all others! How dare he take the liberty!"

"Mrs. Sherwin," Joe said, gravely, but with the twinkle in his eyes and a twitching in the corners of his mouth, "I am surprised at you. You do not suppose for a moment I am the only one favoured by this appeal for pecuniary aid? The worthy and energetic Rector requires a new house. If he may not take a liberty with his friends, whom may he take a liberty with?"

But instead of admitting the rational view as submitted by her husband, Dolly could only exclaim—

"I think I never heard of such an impudent request in all my life!"

And then, as the recollection of the young curate's odious attentions to herself recurred to her, the little woman would have related some instances of duplicity and mischievous interference—perhaps as a justification of her present excitement—to their guest; but Joe said—

"Oh, Frank there knows him. They were fellow-lodgers once, I think; but, as it often happens, a trifle parted them."

"Well," Frank said, quietly, "it wasn't a trifle exactly." Perhaps he recalled the circumstance of the young minister's departure, when he followed his portmanteau downstairs, for he smiled a little, but he reddened slightly notwithstanding.

There are some injuries which the best of us find it hard to forgive, and there are some that, do what we may, we never can pardon. Perhaps Mr. Sherwin had some such feeling, for looking kindly on his little wife, his face became grave and thoughtful, and taking her hand gently in his own, he said—

" I think I can find a better use than this for my spare cash, little woman."

I cannot tell what opinion may prevail as to Joe's decision on the appeal of the new Rector, but as several old mill hands who had worked hard for an honest livelihood, and were now past labour, some being sick, and others perhaps stricken down by domestic trouble or poverty, were always sure of a good Sunday dinner from the Lodge, and of timely assistance in the hour of need, I think if the Reverend Ernest Palethorpe was no better, Joe was no worse, and, maybe, several little homes the brighter and the happier.

" Did you know Mr. Palethorpe's wife ?" Dolly asked of Frank.

" I met her I believe at Brighton, some years ago," he answered; and as one question led to another, he gradually related the meeting on the pier, and the subsequent interview with Major

Maismore and his wife. When he described the Major's personal appearance, Dolly and her husband exchanged glances.

"By the way," he exclaimed, as if suddenly recollecting, "you must remember him, Sherwin. He came in that night you were at my place in Seymour Street. Well, that was the last time I saw him, though I met the lady once or twice afterwards. They disappeared suddenly one day— at least he did; and who or what he was, I never could make out."

"I daresay it was no loss to you," Mr. Sherwin suggested.

"Perhaps not; but he was a pleasant fellow," Frank replied; and turning to Dolly, he continued, "But do you know, Mrs. Sherwin, I once had a more mysterious acquaintance in this very town of Dalesford; for one evening, on going home late, I found a strange figure of a man in a large cloak and sort of Spanish hat, looking at our house. I thought he was a burglar, and addressed him rather sharply, I remember; but he was so polite, or so odd—I really forget which—our meeting ended by my asking him inside, and I passed two of the pleasantest hours I ever had in his company."

"Didn't you know who he was?" Dolly asked.

"Not in the least," Frank said; "and the next

morning he had left the Talbot, where he had been staying, and I never saw or heard of *him* any more."

The morning being fine, Frank accompanied Mr. Sherwin to the town, and as they drove pleasantly along the road to Dalesford, Joe returned to the subject of the Major and his wife.

" It's a strange thing," Frank said ; " but I never could make them out. When I went home one evening to Seymour Street, I learnt that a lady, who had refused to leave her name or card, had called during my absence. I didn't pay much attention to it at the time ; but when the call was repeated I felt annoyed, and desired the servant to say I saw no one who thought proper to adopt that mode of forming acquaintance. However, a few days after I had a letter, signed with the name I had heard the Major address his wife by, and which named a day and hour for an interview. To tell you the truth, I thought it was an appli- cation for pecuniary assistance ; and just then I had not the means to meet such requirements as I supposed they would name."

" Did you see her ?" the other asked.

" Why, you see, I had no help for it," Frank said ; " and I had resolved to state plainly the condition of my own finances, when, to my surprise, no sooner had she entered the room and

taken a seat, than she began to cry—to cry, sir,
like anything."

" What about ?" Joe asked.

" Well," Frank rejoined, " I naturally thought
it was to make her appeal the stronger, and I
began to turn over in my mind what I should say
to her; when, to my still greater astonishment,
she told me in her pretty broken English that she
had ventured to call on me to implore me never to
be induced to play with the Major again."

" Again !" Joe repeated. " Had you played
before, then ?"

" Why, yes," Frank said, and reddened a little ;·
" and I lost confoundedly."

" Naturally," Joe replied. " Well, go on."

" Oh, I have little more to say," he answered.
" She seemed to have some grievance against the
Major, and now and then talked rather incoherently and excitedly, and I was glad when she
went away."

" Why glad ?"

" Well," Frank said, slowly, " I didn't care
much about the acquaintance at the time. You
see, I had had—well, a domestic trouble—and I
left town for a week or so; and when I came back,
I took other apartments."

" Ah ! I see," Mr. Sherwin said. " You refer
to the death of your poor father."

"Why, no," Frank said; "this occurred some time previously to his death. No; I had had—well—a little trouble of my own; we wont refer to it, please."

They were silent for a few seconds, and Joe knew very well then the trouble to which the poor young fellow referred.

"I have sometimes wondered," Frank said, suddenly, "what became of that lady."

"What does become of these poor women?" Joe said, gravely. "A man answering to your description of the Major, and as I saw him on the night you mention, died some years ago in the accident ward of the Manchester Hospital. Probably the Major was an adventurer, and this unfortunate lady might have been his accomplice."

"Likely enough," Frank said. "But I don't think she was altogether a very bad sort. She had certainly the manner and address of a lady, and had the finest eyes I ever saw—of the kind, I mean; and mind, I don't say I like the kind either; not soft and expressive, like—well—your little daughter's; but fierce and shining. I dare almost swear, if you had met her in a dark room, they would have glistened like a panther's."

They remained silent after this, until Mr. Sherwin, reining up the horse before the gate of a

small but pleasant-looking house, with a neat drive
in front, said—

" I am going to see Mr. Worsdale. This is his
house. He has been unwell lately. Will you wait
a minute or two ?"

" No," Frank said. " I would rather see him,
if I may."

" Oh, certainly," Mr. Sherwin said. " By the
way, don't refer to Tim ; it distresses the poor old
fellow."

The house-door was opened by a square-set,
round-faced lad of seventeen, with a good-humoured
though somewhat assertive expression about him.

" Well, mate," Joe said, in his own genial way
to the lad ; " how's the governor by this time ?"

" All right, in the parlour," Phil answered.
" He doesn't say much, you know ; but he's all right.
Should I drive the mare to the stable for you ?"

" This is to be our new accountant," Joe said
to Frank, when they had alighted from the gig, as
he laid his hand kindly on Phil's shoulder. " Yes ;
be off, mate, and take care of the mare's knees and
the gate-posts."

So Phil, not waiting to put on his hat, took the
reins from Mr. Sherwin and drove away as Joe and
his friend entered the house. Frank, with his early
recollection of Mr. Worsdale, was prepared to meet
the same firm and sturdy old fellow he had pre-

viously known. He was a little impressed therefore
by his manner on this occasion. Matthew was
seated with his back to the light, and seemed asleep,
or was perhaps only preoccupied, for on Joe's
touching him on the shoulder gently, and holding
out his hand, as he said in a low but cheery voice—

" Well, sir, how are we this morning ?"

The old gentleman looked up, and recognising
his visitor, inclined his head as he replied—

" Good morning, Joe, good morning."

He regarded Frank steadily for a few seconds,
as if striving to recall his features ; and on Mr.
Sherwin saying—

" I have brought a friend to see you; Mr.
Frank Ossett."

" To be sure," Matthew Worsdale replied, inclining his head as before.   " Mr. Frank Ossett ;
I hope your good father is quite well, sir ?"

Frank looked for a moment surprised and pained ;
but Joe said under his breath—

" He has forgotten ; don't mind him, Frank."
Then he added, as he turned to Mr. Worsdale—

" I have brought you a few strawberries that
Dolly picked this morning. She sends her love,
and hopes you wont go to the mill to-day, if you
don't feel well enough."

" Very proper, very proper—yes, yes. I shall
be down at the mill in the course of an hour,"

Mr. Worsdale replied. "Just make a note of the name of that last consignment of mungo, will you? I have forgotten it."

"It shall be attended to," Joe said, promptly; but he looked very serious as he did so, and added, "But where's Prissy? We want you and Prissy to come home to dinner to-day; the weather is very beautiful, and Mr. Ossett here leaves us to-morrow."

"Well, Joe, that's very kind of you," Mr. Worsdale said. "Prissy may do as she likes; but I am hardly well enough, I think. I am getting old, Mr.—Mr——" he paused a moment, looking at Frank. "I really beg your pardon, but your name has escaped me."

"Ossett, you know—Mr. Frank Ossett," Joe said.

"Quite so—quite so," Matthew said, with the slight inclination of the head again. "Ah, I have known your good father many years—many years. I hope he is quite well."

But Frank comprehending the glance of Mr. Sherwin, turned the conversation by hoping they should have the pleasure of seeing Miss Worsdale.

Mr. Worsdale couldn't say; but if Frank would kindly touch the bell, he would inquire whether she was at home.

Mr. Sherwin, however, by some remark he made diverted the current of his thoughts, ob-

14—2

serving him carefully and with an expression of tender solicitude. Soon afterwards the two friends left the house.

They walked a little way in silence; then Mr. Sherwin said—

" You find him changed, I am afraid ?"

" He is changed," Frank answered, gravely. " Is his memory failing him ?"

" In some respects, yes," Joe answered slowly. " He has had an attack of gout, and it has confined him to the house. He is much better when he can get about."

They walked on again in silence; then Joe said, and his countenance fell, as he spoke in a low and soft voice—

" I sometimes think we shall not have him with us long. He has known some heavy trouble, Frank, and I am afraid it is telling on him now. With the best intentions, we have tried to make his life easy for him, and I think it has been a mistake. I believe he would have been all the better with the cares of business to rouse him."

After another relapse into silence, he said—

" I think he felt the conduct of his son—your old companion, I mean—very keenly. They didn't get on very well together, but the poor old fellow had set much store by him, all unworthy and despicable as he has proved himself to be ; and I believe secretly hoped he would reform, and be a credit to him."

" Where is Tim now ?" Frank asked.

" I don't know," Joe answered, with a tone of irritation in his voice ; " and, as far as he is concerned, I don't care—that! I believe his regiment is, or was lately, at some foreign station, but I really don't know. He wrote to me a whining, miserable letter, some time ago, apparently not aware I was his father's old foreman, entreating to be bought out, and speaking of repentance, and a good deal more of that kind of cant, which I took for what I knew it was worth ; for, take my word, Frank Ossett, if ever there was a worthless young vagabond in this world, it is my brother-in-law, Tim Worsdale ! The little fellow is worth a dozen of him."

" What is Phil going to do ?" Frank inquired.

" When they moved here from Pedlington—near Manchester, you know," Joe said, " we sent Phil to school again. It is remarkable how a year's experience in the world sharpens a lad for school work afterwards ; and as he is a sharp fellow naturally, he got on capitally. He leaves this half, and is to go into the counting-house to learn habits of business."

" And the sister, Priscilla ?" Frank said. " Ah, I remember her before I left Dalesford ; she was a pretty little creature then. I don't think I have seen her since. What of her?"

"Prissy is her father's little housekeeper," Joe answered. "The old gentleman is very fond and proud of her; in fact, she was always her father's favourite."

"Nonsense!" Frank ejaculated. "I mean to say," he added, "I wonder she has not been married, so young and pretty as she is."

"Well," Joe answered, laughing a little, "Miss Priscilla is rather hard to please. She has been a great reader of romances in her time, and her husband must be made to order. I daresay you may have met with such young persons, who build up a world of their own from the pages of fiction, and expect to people it with their own creations also. She has had several offers of marriage, I believe, but has turned a deaf ear. Let us hope she may not eventually resemble the young girl in the story, who went to look for a perfectly straight twig in the osier-bed, and was obliged to be contented with only a crooked one after all."

Having by this time arrived at the gate of the mill, the friends parted, Mr. Sherwin to attend to the business of the day, and Frank Ossett to get through the time in his own pleasant, but purposeless manner. He strolled carelessly up one street and down another, noting the many alterations in the town since he had first known it, till he found himself standing in a sentimental mood before a good-looking house, with a large brass-plate on the gate, signifying it was a select Establishment for Young Ladies.

" Why, bless my life !" he cried, " how the place is changing. I shall forget who I am next. Why, this is old Worsdale House, that I used to walk up and down before so many times, and pretend I was waiting for Tim. What a fool I was, to be sure, in those days."

But he sighed deeply for all that, and turned slowly away. It was about noon when he called at the hotel where he stopped when he was not a visitor at Rosedale, and seating himself in the coffee-room, took up a paper. There were but few persons present at the time, and these he either did not know, or did not care to recognise. But he was conscious that a stalwart, well-dressed young fellow was looking at him very attentively, and at last, when their eyes met, the stranger crossing to him, said—

" Mr. Ossett, surely ! How d'ye do ?"

" I remember the face," Frank said, " but at this moment——"

" Oh, very likely you don't remember me," said the other ; " but we met, you may recollect, when we were in the Torture Chamber in Chancery Lane."

"Where?" Frank asked.

"Well," said the other, laughing, "when we went in for our examination. My name is Todd—Manchester."

Frank remembered him then, and apologising, with his usual pleasant frankness, shook hands cordially.

Mr. Rawley Todd's development in five years was considerable. His hands and feet, which had been so remarkable in the days of his teens, were certainly no less, but his body having increased in bulk, they did not seem so abnormally large as in the years gone by, when he trod on Miss Skimple, and knocked over cups and glasses with his elbows. His countenance, too, had lost some of its diffident and sheepish look, though still marked by an expression of boyish simplicity, which it retained to the end, and his voice had deepened into a strong, unruly bass; but he was a manly-looking fellow, Frank considered, and though a trifle over-dressed, his appearance made a favourable impression.

"I remembered you at once," he said, speaking with the Manchester accent, which became more pronounced as their familiarity increased, "and that you had said once you came from this place. I'm right glad to see you, for sure! You'll dine with me to-day?"

Frank made his excuse, being engaged to return with Mr. Sherwin, and in turn asked what had brought Mr. Todd to Dalesford.

Mr. Todd coloured a little, but he said—

"Oh, a little business, but I return to-night;" so Frank pressed him no further.

They chatted pleasantly for half an hour, and then Mr. Rawley Todd, looking at his watch, said, somewhat nervously, that he must go, as he had a particular appointment; so they shook hands and parted.

Frank had a little business of his own to attend to, and that having been duly discharged, he strolled leisurely onwards, and turned down the street wherein the People's Hall was situated. It seemed quite a modest little building now, among the large factories that had grown up in the neighbourhood, but the place recalled to his mind the evening when he and his thoughtless companion, Tim Worsdale, had brought on themselves the anger of the Hallelujah Band.

"Ah!" Frank said, half aloud, "there's the corner where 'oud Swaddy' gave it to poor Tim. My goodness, how we did catch it!"

Seeing a placard on the door, he crossed the way and read,—" People's Hall. Hallelujah Band. This evening, a Converted Garrotter and Cardsharper will describe his conversion to Grace. Doors open

at Seven.   To commence half-past.   All are welcome.   Glory !"

   " I wonder how much truth that converted sinner will utter to-night !" he said, and walked slowly
on until he reached the brow of the hill that commanded a view of the town.

   " Well," said he, pausing to look back, " Dalesford may have been a pretty place once, when the
river didn't run a dirty purple, and the adjacent
country wasn't spoilt by tall chimneys ; but of all
the hideous towns I ever saw, this is surely the
worst. I'll go away, certainly, to-morrow. I'm
little better than an idiot to come at all. It
always unsettles me, and makes me miserable."

   So he went to the railway station, that was close
by, to study the time-table, and looking at his
watch, found he had still two hours before calling
on Mr. Sherwin as arranged.   He bought a pretty
picture-book for his little favourite, " Dolly," and a
sporting paper for himself, which he proposed to
peruse quietly in the waiting-room ; but seeing a
lady and gentleman there in earnest conversation,
he retired before his presence had been observed.
Then he stood idly watching the railway porters,
who were endeavouring to place some refractory
horses in their travelling vans ; and, after a while,
sauntered townwards again.   He was walking slowly
along, when he noticed Mr. Rawley Todd striding

away rapidly on the other side of the street. He seemed rather excited, for he was smiling pleasantly, and talking to himself almost loud enough to be heard.

"Hollo!" cried Frank, "what's the matter?"

Mr. Todd, thus recalled to himself, ran, I may almost say rushed, across the road and shook Frank cordially by the hand, telling him how delighted he was to see him.

As it was little more than an hour since they had parted, Frank was at a loss to account for this strange behaviour; but he was still more surprised when Mr. Todd, again shaking him by the hand, exclaimed—

"You don't know how pleased I am to have met you! Will you do me a favour?"

"What do you mean?" Frank asked.

"Will you have a bottle of champagne with me?" Rawley asked, looking red and excited.

"What the devil's the matter, man?" Frank said, after a pause. "Are you going off your head?"

"My dear old fellow!" Mr. Todd exclaimed, in another burst of excitement, "I shouldn't wonder! Let's go to the Talbot!"

"I think you had better not go there again to-day, Todd," Frank said, gravely. "What have you been about?"

"I give you my word, Mr. Ossett," Mr. Todd said, in an injured tone, "I have touched nothing. I own I am excited! I am overjoyed! Come and have a bottle of fiz, old fellow, or I shall do something desperate!"

"Now look here, Todd," Frank observed; "I have never seen you like this before. Keep yourself quiet. We shall have the people looking at us directly. Tell me what's the matter, if you like, but do keep yourself quiet."

"Come and have a bottle of fiz, old man," Mr. Todd insisted, "to wish me luck!—don't say no, there's a good fellow!"

Seeing he was resolute on this point Frank yielded, and they walked together to the hotel. But though Mr. Todd's manner was more subdued, it was not less strange. He led the way to a private room, and Frank prepared himself to listen.

"Wait till that confounded waiter's out of the room," Mr. Rawley Todd said. "Now then, you sir," he added to that official, who had entered with the wine, "what are you waiting for?"

The waiter submitted the probability of his being required to draw the cork.

"Cork? No!" Mr. Todd rejoined. "I can do that! I've drawn more corks than ever you'll see!"

" I am the happiest fellow, and the luckiest!"
he went on when they were left alone, and had
finished their first glass.

" What do you mean?" Frank asked again.

" I say, sir, the happiest and the luckiest!"
Mr. Todd repeated; " and she is the sweetest and
the prettiest."

" She? Oh, that's it, is it?" Frank sagely remarked. " Ah, you needn't say any more."

" My dear friend!" Mr. Todd said, pathetically,
" don't think worse of me because I am making a
fool of myself "—(here he wiped an eye with his
forefinger); " but you don't know how happy I am!"

" I'm very glad to hear it, my boy," Frank
replied, cordially. " I hope she may deserve the
truth and love of such a good fellow, as I feel
sure you are."

" I hope I may deserve her love!" Rawley said,
simply; " but I will try to—I *will* try to!"

" I am sure of that," Frank said, kindly and
gently; for he felt touched by the simplicity of the
great fellow by his side, whose large hand trembled
in the excitement he was under; " I am quite sure
of that; and I am sure you will, too."

" Do you think so, Ossett? Do you really
think so?" Rawley said. " Let's have another
bottle, eh?"

But Frank declined, entreating his friend to be

careful; and learning from him that he had arranged to leave Dalesford for Manchester that evening, accompanied him to the station, and remained with him there until he had taken his seat in the carriage.

" But there's one thing," Frank said, as he stood on the step, wringing his friend's hand, as the train began to move slowly away, " now you haven't told me who she is ?"

" Never you mind that, old man !" Todd said. " All in good time. Enough for me—I am accepted !"

And the train steamed out of the station.

" Poor old fellow !" Frank said, as he turned away. " I sincerely hope he may never know what it is to be disappointed."

That same evening, as Frank sat in the pleasant drawing-room at Rosedale, talking with his friends of the events of the day—but suppressing all mention of Mr. Todd's confidence—and as Mr. Rawley Todd himself, looking like a man and feeling like a boy, was in a state of joyous excitement, scarcely knowing whether to laugh or to cry, while Mr. Worsdale was listening placidly as his pretty daughter sang his favourite songs to him, inclining his head from time to time by way of approval, but saying nothing; and as Phil was practising on the local

ground for a cricket match that was to take place
on the morrow, a miserable-looking creature, having
the appearance of a tramp, with clothes so be-
daubed with mud that it would have been difficult
to distinguish their original colour, crawled out of
a ditch that separated a small coppice from the
pathway of one of the high roads in the pleasant
county of Kent. There were no houses visible, or
those only of the poorest description, such as are occupied by the commonest of agricultural labourers;
but the man looked cautiously on each side
before he ventured to emerge wholly from the
place where he seemed to have been lying as if
for concealment; and then, apparently satisfied he
was quite alone, he started on his journey. From
his shambling and halting gait he was probably
sadly footsore and leg-weary; but lame and fagged
and jaded as he undoubtedly was, he flung himself
over a gate with much alacrity at the sound of a
horse's hoofs on the road behind him, and lay in
the long grass of the meadow until the horseman
had passed. Then he hurried on as best he might,
but still occasionally looking back, as if in a very
fever of fear and miserable apprehension. As he
approached a small village which lay at the foot
of a hill he would have to surmount, he paused for
a moment, wistfully gazing at a group of children
at play, and offered one of them a penny for a

large wedge of bread and bacon which the child
had in its hands.   But the little boy, having stared
at the stranger for a few seconds in silent dismay,
evidently regarded him as one of the dangerous
classes, and, setting up a loud howl, fled homewards.
Arrived at the summit of the hill, the traveller
paused again for breath, and looked about him.

It was a beautiful evening, in the early part of
June.   Below him lay the peaceful village he had
passed through ; before him was the large unexplored
world, with its dangers, its difficulties, and its
thousand troubles ; with its suspicions and doubts
of such as he was, and with its cordial welcome to
success, and friendly greeting for all that do not
require it.   He turned again, and then pursued his
journey.   A few yards further, and removed a little
from the high road, stood the village church, with
its old grey, square tower, to which the parasitical
ivy was clinging with a pertinacious orthodoxy, that
seemed to bind together such parts as were breaking
away, or as if to conceal some of the flaws and
fissures in the construction of the Establishment.
A footpath ran through the churchyard to the fields
and hills far away, and, branching off at one corner,
communicated by a neat gate with the pleasant
garden of the Rectory.   Small as the building itself
was, it was still snug and picturesque, and quite in
harmony with the peaceful scene in which it lay.

The traveller passed through the turnstile, and following the footpath, paused for a moment or so to look over the little gate of the Rectory garden. A lady, somewhat broad in face and figure, was tying up the flowers, and not having heard the tramp's approach, by reason of his walking on the grass to ease his wounded feet, was considerably startled when, looking up, she saw his wan and toil-worn face within a few yards of her own.

"Good gracious!" she exclaimed, "whatever do you want here? Go away at once, or I'll call the dog! Here, Fi! Fi! Fi!"

A fat and foolish-looking little Spaniel, with a short and blunt nose and long ears, appeared in answer to this appeal, and having barked feebly once, wagged his little tail and lay down to sleep.

The tramp told a brief, sad tale of suffering and hunger, and begged for a crust of bread and drink of water, for God's sake.

"How dare you come here?" the lady said. "If the Rector was at home, he'd send you to prison at once!"

The man said he meant no harm; he only asked a trifling assistance to help him on the way; but the lady replied that the Rector objected to indiscriminate relief, and disapproved of beggars in any form, and again desired the tramp to go away, or she should be under the necessity of setting the dog on him.

He said nothing to this, but retiring a few yards, sat wearily down on an old gravestone, and, in that blank state of mind that results often from over-fatigue or a dearth of food, fell to idly tracing out the inscription, well-nigh obliterated by time, which set forth the manifold virtues of the one lying below, whose Christian love and charity were as cold now as the rest of the dead—or as some of the living.

Considerably relieved by the tramp's withdrawal, the lady trilled a sportive lay, and returned to the care of her flowers, until aroused by a voice saying—

" Wifey ! wifey !"

She looked up, and saw a full pale face with a sickly smile, playing at what little children call " bo-peep," behind the curtain of the open window.

" Who is that little man I see ?" the lady rejoined, falling in at once with the humour of the innocent sport.

" Wifey-pifey, poor hubby wants his tea, wifey-pifey !" the voice from the window replied, assuming the injured tone of a pet child, that cannot at once obtain what the dear little thing desires; on which the lady gambolled up to the open window, archly shaking her long curls, and looking full of girlish mischief.

Here the mirthful Rector took a kiss from the

broad face presented to him for the purpose, with
the rosy mouth (I believe that is the correct description of that pleasant feature of a guileless nature)
pursed up in a provoking and irresistible fashion ;
and shortly afterwards he appeared in the garden,
with a dressing-gown and a broad-brimmed straw
hat substituted for the ecclesiastical attire, which
became him so well, and added so much to the
weight of his ministrations.

I think the Rector's lady—she was slightly taller
and certainly broader than her husband—took this
occasion, as she fondly leant on his arm, to inform
him of her recent interview with the tramp, who
was now idly picking the moss off the stone, and
absently running his fingers along the grooves of
the lettering, for the Rector, assuming an austere
tone, quite at variance with his previous gentle
dalliance, exclaimed—

"I cannot permit this ! I will not suffer this !
Where is he ? Hollo, you, sir !" he cried, in his
deepest and choicest tones—those which he seemed
to keep for special occasions, when more than
ordinary solemnity was required—as soon as he
descried where the miserable tramp was sitting,
"this will not do ! You must not be there, you
know ! Leave my churchyard this moment !"

He was very hungry, the tramp said, and weary,
with no place to lay his head, and no money to buy

15—2

a piece of bread, and would be grateful for a scrap of anything in the way of food !

But the Rector reminded him that state of affairs was not his (the Rector's) fault; that he was not called upon to help all the vagrant fellows who thought proper to live by mendicancy ; that beggars of all kinds ought to be discouraged, and that he wouldn't—he would *not*—permit that kind of thing there; and that if the tramp did not immediately transfer himself to the adjoining parish, he should call out the local constabulary and have him removed.

At this the vagrant seeing that that broad human sympathy, of which he might have heard in better days, and of which the Rector occasionally read, I daresay, on a Sunday, as illustrated by a certain traveller who took a journey to Jericho, like that precious metal that men will risk their safety and their lives to obtain, was not always to be found in the very places of all others where we should go to look for it, arose from his seat and was about to limp away, when the other called to him—

" Hi ! stop a moment. You have doubtless been a great sinner—this may prove serviceable to you."

As the reverend gentleman put his hand in his pocket the tramp, naturally enough, inferred that pecuniary assistance was at hand, and hopefully retraced his steps towards the little gate.

" Fellow sinner," said the Rector, with a self-complacent air, and in a soft and pleasant voice, as he placed a small leaflet in the tramp's extended hand, " read this. I trust it may bring forth fruit meet for repentance."

" Good God!" cried the tramp, holding on by the little gate as he looked full in the Rector's face for the first time—" It's Ernest Palethorpe !"

Allowing for any difference that may exist between the clocks of Kent and Yorkshire, simultaneously with the excited exclamation of the miserable creature in the peaceful churchyard of Heron's Mount, and which had so startled the Rector and his good lady—Mr. Thomas Stepper, bill-sticker, pigeon-fancier, dog-stealer, swindler, thief, and ruffian, with a dirty wisp of white neckcloth twisted round his bull-neck, though he wore a coat of a sporting cut and cord trousers, and with his usual hang-dog expression of face more pronounced, if possible, than ever, stepped clumsily on the platform of the People's Hall in Dalesford, to describe in a coarse and thick voice, with many pious ejaculations, and with the assumption of much self-abasement, how a Garrotter and a Cardsharper was " converted unto Grace."

CHAPTER XI.

THE LAST STAGE.

AS it not the great Napoleon, who, in those terrible last hours of Waterloo, when his gallant cavalry charged again and again—and still in vain—the firm, imperturbable squares of British Infantry, complained that the English did not know when they were beaten? Have we not read how those brave French troopers galloped round and round the quadrangle of Living Death, vainly striving to find a weak point, while at every deadly discharge of the heavy musket, the flower of the valiant horsemen rolled from their saddles, leaving the noble chargers to career, frightened and riderless, over the plains of blood and carnage? Surely a terrible and a grand spectacle, that impetuous onslaught of the armed troopers on the one side, and the calm, pale, impassive courage of the Anglo-Saxon Infantry men on the other, awaiting the furious charge with the fixed bayonet, and at the word of command dealing death and defeat to the mounted warriors. There is a strangely resolute and self-reliant air in those masses of our Foot soldiery, moving with the precision of a vast machine, and yet composed of so many thousands of individual hopes, doubts, thoughts, passions, and affections. Divested of the glitter, pomp, and romance which still cling to the Cavalry hero, there is an air of quiet and resolute purpose about them which the others seem to lack. We cannot see them at drill or manœuvring on a field, and not marvel at the courage, endurance, and discipline of those red-coated fellows, that calmly withstand the rush of Cavalry or boldly storm the fortress, with the cannon flashing destruction in their ranks, driving the gunners from their post, and planting their country's colours there.

Yet, I am constrained to admit, that taken by himself and in his leisure moments, the private of Infantry is not interesting. He is frequently little more than a mere lad, and not seldom appears under-sized. His costume is not becoming when isolated, nor is the fit of the garment unexceptionable. He seems to have been sharing the quarters of a brother soldier, who is also a bigger one, and by mistake to have put on his clothes. There are creases and puckers in his coarse red jacket, arising from a super-fluity of material; and his dark pepper-and-salt trousers frequently commence at his armpits and terminate in the mud—while of his hands the finger-

nails are alone visible.   How is this, I have asked
myself; cannot the soul of the hero of Foot conde-
scend to the details of dress? or does Britannia,
like some mothers we have known, lavish her attention on the more brilliant of her warlike children,
giving them horses to ride and becoming clothes to
wear, while the others are left to shift for themselves,
or are put into suits too large, as if to admit of their
growing?   That big brother of his in the Dragoons
is a smart fellow; he may seem in his shell-jacket,
perhaps, unduly long in the leg, but the white
leather gloves and the clanking spurs, associated as
they are with the gallant war-steed, that says " Ha!
ha!" when he hears the trumpet of battle, have
such a bold, daring, and heroic character about
them, that Mary Ellen may well be pardoned if she
tarries with the perambulator to look back at the
manly figure, or allows her tender charges to fall
asleep with their heads over the side, while Mars
stoops to pleasant parlance with Venus.   But our
Infantry man is shorn of all this romance and
chivalry; and then I cannot blame the mistress who
gives Mary Ellen notice to leave, for talking to
soldiers in the park.   I cannot understand any
young person with a well-regulated mind, and with
an eye to colour and costume, demeaning herself by
a friendly colloquy with such an object.   I am
afraid her principles cannot be sound.   I fear she

must be of a visionary and fanciful turn, and invests with dignity and grace that grotesque figure in a dull red and black pepper-and-salt, who is so sadly deficient in both those qualities. Certainly he sticks his absurd little cap on one side; he has a self-conscious air, and he swaggers,—but it will not do. Whatever he may be, at least he doesn't look a hero. He is only five feet seven at most; his face is pimply, and his hair, though plentifully greased, will not curl. His boots, of the Blucher variety, are broad and splay; he is not impressive, he is only pretentious; and though he smiles on Mary Ellen, and whispers low, smokes a short pipe, and raps his capacious trousers with a cheap cane, Private Blank of the —th (off duty) is an object and a sham.

On the forenoon of the day of that little incident in the churchyard, several of these heroes were variously occupied in the barracks of one of the garrison towns of Kent. Groups in different parts of the yard were performing evolutions, in obedience to an inarticulate and spasmodic word of command from the officer in charge; others were looking out of the windows of the buildings in a state of undress, and soothing themselves with an early pipe. The sentinels, fully equipped, were patrolling the short flagstone pavement adapted expressly for their use, and looking solemn and mysterious. An occasional trumpeter appeared, and, having sounded a few notes on his instrument, withdrew. Two officers, out of uniform, drove in a dogcart through the gates of the yard chatting pleasantly, and acknowledging briefly the salute of the sentry.

"A jolly life that of the military," a bystander, with the appearance of a civilian, remarked to another person also looking on, as they stood watching the well-appointed vehicle leave the barrack yard.

"Which I had always a fancy for it myself," the other replied.

Just then three military gentlemen, in full uniform, appeared from a building close by. One was clearly in authority, for the other two, standing side by side before him, went through several movements in obedience to his order. Then he suddenly cried, what sounded like "Wick ma'!" and the trio walked out of the barrack yard.

"What are they up to now?" the first speaker inquired of the sentinel on guard.

"Pursuit of deserter," he replied; and immediately resumed his walk to and fro.

I may as well confess at once, that in such cases my sympathy has always been with the fugitive; and I admit, if he were to come my way, I should be strongly inclined to stow him in a garden-house or a cellar, till the danger was past; or lend him an old coat or a wig, if I had one, to enable him to baffle pursuit; that is, of course, so long as I believed his fault did not extend beyond simple desertion.

I think better and wiser than I, have derived some satisfaction in seeing the object of pursuit elude his hunters when the odds are in their favour, especially when we take into consideration the agony of fear, the miserable suspense, and the physical efforts involved. We may imagine some poor, inexperienced lad, having enlisted in a moment of thoughtlessness or resentment, or dazzled by the glowing picture of a life of jollity and martial glory as presented by the recruiting officer, waking at last from the hollow dream, repentant and home-sick, with an irresistible yearning for the old roof-tree and the cottage fireside, where the old father and ailing mother sit, sorrowfully wishing for their foolish boy's return; and how, at certain times of the year, pure and happy associations rush back on his memory, until his barrack becomes a prison, and the regular routine of duty an ever-recurring punishment; until at last, the impulse becoming stronger and firmer, he yields to the temptation, and eluding pursuit for a while, is taken back degraded and disgraced, to learn what further humiliation awaits a soldier guilty of desertion.

Ah! it was well for that limping and half-famished tramp, who had called the Reverend Ernest

Palethorpe by his name, that the Rector of Heron's Mount was not aware how he had let himself out of the barrack window the previous night, and slunk away through the foss-dyke, and under cover of the walls, making off for the open country with the energy of desperation, across fields of long mowing grass, or young corn, bursting through hedges and crawling up the wet ditches to soil his clothes and obliterate every vestige, as far as possible, of the service he was disgracing. If that proverbial little bird, whose mission seems to be to make privileged communication, could have winged its flight to the Rectory that sweet June evening, and whispered into the car of the interesting Martha tying up the flowers, that the miserable creature sitting on the tombstone was a criminal, whose inevitable doom, according to the popular belief in our nursery days, was death at the hands of his comrades, I have no doubt she would have held him in converse till such time as he could be safely handed over to the proper authorities; but, fortunately for him, the Rector's objection to mendicancy, when referring to his own pocket or larder, befriended him on this occasion, and he had limped off as quickly as he could under the advantage of night, putting as many miles as possible between himself and his pursuers.

It was about a fortnight afterwards that Mr.

Sherwin said, as he prepared to leave home for the business of the day—

" I think, Dolly, you had better go with me to Dalesford this morning. Your father wasn't so well last night, and may like to see you."

" Nothing the matter, Joe, is there?" his wife asked in a tone of alarm.

" Nothing to frighten you, my dear," Joe said gravely, " but I am afraid he is breaking."

Dolly was silent, as was her wont when anything of importance seemed to require her attention, but she was quite ready to accompany her husband, and seemed earnest and thoughtful.

As they were about to leave the gate Phil arrived, out of breath from running up the hill. He had come over by an early train, he said, for Mr. Worsdale had been taken ill in the night, and Prissy was in a state of terrible anxiety that her sister should be present, without any loss of time.

Joe drove rapidly to the town, and they said but little on the way. They found Matthew Worsdale lying in the bed, quiet and breathing regularly, but apparently unconscious. His eyes were closed, but he did not seem to be sleeping. They learnt from Prissy, who, with a frightened face and crying bitterly, had led them into another room, that Matthew had retired to rest the previous night as usual, apparently no worse, as far as she herself

could judge, though Joe, she admitted, had asked
her two or three questions before leaving for home,
which at the time she scarcely heeded.   They had
been startled some time afterwards by the sound of
a fall in her father's room, and hastening to learn
the cause, had found Mr. Worsdale lying on the
floor.   He seemed to have risen from the bed and
to have partly dressed himself, but his clothes had
been put on carelessly and out of order ; as if
by some one half-asleep, or not quite conscious of
what he was doing.   He did not seem to have
injured himself in any way, and she believed he
must have had a fit.   The medical man had been
promptly sent for, but he had been called into the
country late that same evening and had not, up
to that time, returned.

"He mustn't be left a moment, my dear," Dolly
quietly said, "and we will take it by turns to sit up
with him ; I'll begin to-night—you must have some
rest—and you can take your turn to-morrow."

She took her place by the side of the old man's
bed, and stooping down to move aside the white
hair that had fallen over the furrowed forehead,
kissed him tenderly.   Matthew Worsdale opened
his eyes, and after lying silently for a few seconds,
said with difficulty—

"Has Tim come ?"

"Not yet, father," Dolly said gently after a

moment's pause; " but I daresay he wont be long."

"Oh !" the old man said, " when he comes, let me see him, will you?" and he closed his eyes again.

The two sisters looked at one another in silence, and with an expression of surprise in their faces. Seeing that Matthew remained quite placid, at a gesture from Dolly, Prissy followed her from the room.

" Prissy," Dolly said in her low, gentle voice, as she took her sister's head tenderly between her hands and pressed her lips to the other's ear, " we must try to bear this bravely. You will soon lose your best friend, my darling; this is our father's deathbed."

Shortly afterwards the doctor arrived, travel-stained and jaded, from his night's duty; but he had lost no time, and gravely and carefully he observed the sick man, as he stood by the bedside.

Do our physicians and surgeons fully recognise, I wonder, the importance which we, who stand by, attach to the slightest variation of expression in their faces ? How a gesture or a glance can carry hope or bring despair; how every word they utter then is treasured up, and every hesitation in their speech carefully weighed and measured ?

Dolly, who listened to his directions earnestly,

said but little, but her sister awaited the doctor's coming downstairs, and weeping sadly, begged him to give her a word of hope.

" Your father has such an excellent constitution, and is in such good hands, Miss Worsdale, we may well hope for the best," he had said as he left the house; and in her usually hopeful and impulsive mood she interpreted this into a favourable view of her father's case, and hurried to impart the good tidings to her sister.

With little variation, Mr. Worsdale lay in this state for several days, his daughters watching him by turns at night; though for the matter of that, when poor Prissy, tired out with grieving and broken rest had fallen asleep in her armchair by the bed-side, she didn't know that the footstep that had become mixed up with her dreams was the cautious tread of the self-denying little woman whom she supposed to be asleep in another room. and whose first consideration had ever been for others, to add to their happiness or to lessen their sufferings.

Matthew spoke more rarely now, and in a more feeble voice; but it was still the same question—had Tim come? and still Dolly gave the same gentle, soothing answer; and the old man would close his eyes quietly, as if comforted by that assurance from her lips.

" Ah, Prissy ! If Tim only could come !" Dolly

had said. " How little that miserable boy knows what comfort he would bring to his poor father !"

The first time after his fall that Matthew showed any interest in what was passing near him, was when Mr. Sherwin, in consideration of his little girl's often repeated entreaty that she might see dear mamma, had brought the little thing with him. Dolly had taken her to the sick-room to see poor grandpapa, as she said, and the old man waking then, or seeming to do so, his eyes rested on the little child.

He looked at her long and wistfully at first, and then indicating by a gesture that he wished to be raised in his bed, they supported him with pillows, and he said, but with difficulty—

" Dolly, my dear, is that you ? You are growing a great girl now—you must try to grow a good girl too—you will have to go to school soon, my dear."

To Prissy's look of surprise, Dolly herself replied by a gesture, for she knew her father's mind was wandering back to the days when she herself was a helpless little creature, like her own little one sitting on the bed.

Matthew sat gazing sadly on the little child, and his face assumed a troubled look, as if he were endeavouring to recall something he had forgotten, and then he sighed heavily and lay back again.

He rambled in his talking a great deal that day.

From one or two expressions he seemed to be
thinking of the fire at the mill, for he said more
than once—

"It's in Number Four, they say—Number Four;"
and then he would lie silently again for some time,
but never failing to repeat—

"When he comes let me see him, will you?"

All this time Mr. Sherwin carefully attended to
the business of the firm, saying very little—though
it was soon noised about how ill the senior partner
was—staying at the house as late as possible every
evening, and returning early in the morning; when
Dolly would meet him at the door with intelligence
of the patient's condition.

One morning she was absent for so long a time
that Prissy, who had been left in charge of the sick-
room, taking advantage of her father's sleeping
placidly, followed her sister downstairs. Dolly was
seated in a chair in the small parlour; she had
been crying, and was looking scared and troubled.
Her husband was pacing the room with an irritation
of manner unusual for him.

"Joe! dear Joe!" Prissy heard her sister say in
a tone of remonstrance, "at a time like this we
must not give way to any feeling of resentment.
Let us forgive, dear Joe, and try to forget, in the
face of the great sorrow so near at hand."

"I cannot be the hypocrite, Dolly, to say I

forgive a wrong like that," Mr. Sherwin answered; "and more than that, I do not see why—remembering the results as I do—why I should try to do so. And I felt the safest course I could adopt was to come away as soon as possible, and tell you of our meeting."

He sat down again in the chair he had risen from in his irritation, and beat his foot angrily on the floor.

" Joe, my dearest husband and best friend," his wife said, placing her arms round his neck and laying her frank and true face near to his, " you will think better of this. God has been very good to us, dear, for we are together. Malice and calumny have not prevailed against His good providence. We can afford then to bury the past in the blessing of the present and the hope of the future."

Joe drew her to his side—he was silent a while—having a little struggle, perhaps, with his angry feelings; but he kissed her tenderly, and said with a sigh of relief—

" It shall be as you say, my darling—at least, I will do my best. God bless you, Dolly."

Matthew Worsdale lay all that day apparently unconscious of what was passing. When his eyes were not closed as in slumber, he seemed to be looking vacantly before him, as a person does who walks

16—2

in his sleep. He spoke but seldom now, taking such medicine or food as was offered to him passively, but without any indication that he was conscious of doing so. At long intervals he would utter a few broken sentences, but they were in so indistinct a voice, that though those about him strained their hearing to the utmost, they could scarcely catch the words. Who can guess what the thoughts or the dreams of a dying person are? Who shall say that, while the physical nature is sinking out of us, our immortal part is not in the fullest life? And that behind the glazed eyes and impassive face the mind is not still vigorous and active, though we cannot see its operations under the mask of the slowly changing features?

The doctor had bade them be prepared for the worst, though he added that the strong frame and the resolute will of the man, now lying weak and helpless, would be subdued only after a stubborn resistance. But during the night a visible change had passed over Matthew Worsdale, and they felt that the morning, which had broken in the rich beauty of a summer sunrise, would be the last that would dawn for him on earth.

His family had gathered round his bed, tenderly watching that stern and brave old face slowly, slowly yielding before the stronger power approaching. He had had a brief sleep, and opening his eyes seemed to be more collected, and as he looked on the sorrowing faces of his children, there was a tender recognition in his glance ; and then the troubled expression returned, as if all that he sought for was not there. He seemed to be making a strong effort to put the oftentimes repeated question once more— but Dolly knew the words he would have spoken, and she answered softly, as she reverently kissed the old man's face—

" Yes, father dear, he *has* come at last !—and in time, dear father, in time ! Thank God !—thank God !"

And then gently moving the curtain aside, his miserable, foolish son, subdued and penitent, praying his dying father to forgive him for the grief and trouble he had caused, knelt down by the bed, while Dolly tenderly placed the old man's hand upon his head. And thus, with almost a smile, holding her gentle hand in his, and with his last look on earth fixed on his faithful daughter's loving face, Matthew Worsdale died.

CHAPTER XII.

THE END OF THE JOURNEY.

SO they laid the stout old heart to rest, and a plain massive stone marks the place where the stubborn, brave, honest, and arbitrary old Englishman sleeps his last peaceful sleep, after the troubles and hardships of his long journey. They knew and they respected his earnest, simple nature too well, to place any inscription but the plainest and the briefest on his grave. His indomitable courage under difficulties, his resolute industry and perfect integrity, were treasured in a tender living memory that recalled him always at his best, and mourned for him with love and reverence.

Our little Priscilla, with the wayward impulse of her nature, for some time afterwards visited the burial-place every morning, and left a little nosegay of freshly-gathered flowers on the old man's grave; but as the season changed and the rain fell, or the flowers became more and more scarce, her visits were less frequent, and this demonstrative regret wore itself out.

Her sister Dolly, who had little of the parade of sentiment, tied such flowers as she gathered into little bunches for the children, who standing by her knee would ask her to tell them again the story—the story of the poor brave boy that, industrious and honest, lived to earn the love of those who rightly knew him, and the respect of all good men. They were never tired of hearing her simple story, nor she of telling it; and when sometimes in her low, soft voice, she described how, with a clear conscience and a firm faith, he had met the inevitable end with a gentle smile, and the little ones had grown sorrowful for poor Grandpapa, I have known Joe walk to the window and look into the garden, and Uncle Phil say he would take a walk.

It was about a month after the funeral that Mr. Sherwin, accompanied by Mr. Tim Worsdale, left Dalesford by an early train for Liverpool. Mr. Tim, whose persevering efforts to cultivate a whisker and moustache, seemed in a fair way to be rewarded with success, and whose hair, by Mr. Sherwin's own suggestion, had been suffered to grow rather long behind, looked a very different figure from the unhappy tramp who had sat listlessly on the grave-stone of the churchyard of the Reverend Ernest Palethorpe, or from the private in the Infantry with the badly-fitting clothes, who, chirruping with his lips and teeth, had talked pleasant nonsense to Mary

Ellen in the park. He had given Dolly more than
once, during Mr. Sherwin's absence in Dalesford, a
harrowing description of life in barracks, and the
privations and hardships that had driven him at last
to attempt an escape from it. It reflected much
credit on his powers of graphic narrative, and if I
could only remember it correctly would gladly introduce it here. But as he had told the story also
to his sister Priscilla, and again to Phil, and as each
version had differed from the preceding one in
many details, and the last description was the most
vivid, I am afraid of becoming confused, and of
stating what is not quite accurate.

I do not think Tim shared this scruple, and from
the silence of Dolly on this subject one might suspect what was her view also. His account of how—
dreading detection—he had ripped off the narrow
stripes from his military trousers, and during one
night had placed the red undress jacket, which
must have been certain betrayal had he continued
to wear it, on the pole of a scarecrow in a field,
taking therefrom a tattered hat and coat in exchange,
astonished Prissy and amused Phil ; and when once,
after supper, but always in Mr. Sherwin's absence,
when his tongue had been loosened, and his imagi-
nation stimulated by the enjoyment of the sub-
stantial comforts which were never wanting in Rosedale Lodge, he described how he had lain in a muddy

ditch, while these in pursuit had passed close by, not two yards off, and had even stepped over the very place where he was concealed, with their muskets loaded and cocked, and prepared to shoot down the first unhappy creature who looked like a deserter, Phil's breathing came quick and short, and Prissy cowered with terror. For, as some one has sagely remarked that no man becomes suddenly bad, so, I submit, no one becomes, on the other hand, unexpectedly good, no matter what his bitter experience may have been, or how severe his peni-tence just before; and, as we have seen that Tim, from the first hour of our acquaintance with him, had always been possessed of the devil of lying, so we must not suppose that such an Evil Influence would suffer himself to be ejected after so long an occupa-tion, as if he had been merely a tenant-at-will.

Whatever the adornments, from time to time, of Tim's narrative may have been, one thing was clear, that on Mr. Sherwin's return home late one night from the sick-house in Dalesford, he had found a miserable, abject wretch, half-clad and almost famished, cringing near the garden-gate, and en-treating him to have compassion on the son of his father's old friend.

"I could not drive him out then, Dolly," Joe had said to his wife, "so I promised him food and shelter for that night at least; and in the morning

I only consented to harbour him for a while, on the condition of his strict silence on all subjects in which we have an interest. Failing that, I threatened to communicate with the authorities and to hand him over to them."

This, Mr. Sherwin further explained, had been absolutely essential, for on Mr. Tim recognising in the husband of his sister the former foreman of his father's mill, he began to regard as a right on his side what was really a concession on the other; and with the sense of security which he experienced, would soon have made himself quite comfortable in his present quarters, after his own fashion, as if there were no such things in the world as handcuffs or guardrooms.

So Mr. Sherwin (or " Joe," as Dolly still called him) rightly or wrongly——in whichever way you are pleased to regard his conduct——concealed this young scapegrace, and fed and clothed him until such time as he could dispose of him in safety; and, I believe, as long as Dolly would have come to thank him, with tears in her gentle brown eyes, for his forbearance towards the worthless lad, and for his considerate love for her in her sorrow for her father's death, he would have done far more than that, and not have been ashamed of it either.

But one thing Joe would not do: he would not sit in the same room, nor hold any communication whatever with Tim Worsdale, excepting on such matters as were unavoidable. He refused to hear any account of his previous life, or to listen to any justification of his conduct. He had told him, sternly and briefly, he must thank Dolly's forgiving nature for everything; for that he himself would have nothing to say to or do with him; and the next time Mr. Sherwin addressed him was on the night before their departure, when he had told him to be prepared for the journey to Liverpool in the morning; adding that he should be started in the world again; that the past should be no bar to his advancement, if he would only have the wisdom to profit by the experience of it, but that from that time forth they would hold no further communication. And I believe they never did; though many years afterwards Dolly received a letter from New Zealand, in which the writer spoke of his prospects not being so brilliant as he had been led to expect when he migrated there from Australia; and that he had some thoughts of returning to the old country, if he could raise a sum sufficient for the purpose, admitting the weakness of wishing that his " last resting-place on earth should be in the land of his fathers."

What became of him eventually I cannot say; but some years subsequently, a person of the same name, and, allowing for time and its many changes, not unlike the Tim Worsdale I once knew, kept a small newsvendor's and tobacconist's shop in a narrow street in Liverpool, having married the widow of the former proprietor; and, I believe to this day, Dolly knew something about it, and perhaps Joe also; though the subject was not mentioned by either.

One fine morning Miss Priscilla told her sister how it was she had been induced to consider Mr. Rawley Todd's proposal in a favourable light.

"For you know, dear," she said sentimentally, "I had determined never to marry while poor papa lived—and I never did; and though poor, dear Rawley is not quite what my girlish fancy pictured, still I am sure he is a most worthy creature, and I might do much worse. He came, dear, to see poor papa on business when Mr. Spink was ill, and thus we renewed the acquaintance. (You must remember him, dear, that night of the tea-drinking; the last we had before the fire, when that stupid Ernest Palethorpe wanted to make a speech, or something of the kind, and poor papa wouldn't let him—you remember poor Rawley, surely, treading on dear old Skimple, and how we laughed, at least how I did?) Well, so we met, and then he came again, you know, and that is how it began."

And so in due time they were married, and lived in Manchester, or near it, and Rawley's simple face

beams with pride and pleasure, and his big hands
and feet beat in sympathy, as his pretty, blue-eyed
little wife sings " Deh non voler" (" It was poor,
dear papa's favourite, you know, dear!") or, " Ah,
che la morte," before a circle of admiring friends.

Joe Boothroyd was right, when some years before
he had told the Reverend Ernest Palethorpe that,
without any of the acquirements we call accomplishments, his little favourite Phil had all the
qualities that go to make the successful man of
business; for with the sturdy square frame that
had given such individuality to his father's presence,
Phil inherited also the energy and promptitude, the
foresight and carefulness, which had characterised
Matthew Worsdale's commercial career. After he
had obtained his majority, Mr. Sherwin made him
his junior partner; so the old firm of " Sherwin
and Worsdale" still remains.

I was glad to learn that, after the demise of her
friend and patroness, Lady Petitoe, our poor Skimple
found herself well provided for. She had been a
selfish, calculating person, it cannot be denied; and
one who was much given to the utterance of plati-
tudes and respectable twaddle; affecting a great
deal which no doubt she did not feel, and guided
by self-interest in all her actions. But she was a
lonely old woman, with very few, if any, friends;
and with no companion but the constant memory of

a bitter wrong, to remind her ever of the hollowness
of the world's love and friendship; and we will not
be hard on her if she soured a little under the
recollection. She had been a comfort and a help to
her feeble employer, and it was but right she should
have some recompense for the unutterable boredom
she must have endured, and the calm self-restraint
she exhibited under it. Finding the house her late
friend had devised to her was too large and too
expensive for her requirements, she decided to let it,
and sojourned at several pleasant and quiet seaside
and inland places, (where competent Respectability,
and the Gentility that has means, resort for change
of air and scene,) with a view no doubt to dissipate
the grief she might be supposed to feel for her
deceased friend. When the proper period for
mourning had expired she got over her affliction,
and seemed to take life pretty easily; looking up her
former acquaintances who had thriven in the world,
and politely ignoring those whose course had been
in the opposite direction. I cannot tell through
what channel the intelligence had been conveyed
to her, but she had certainly heard of the altered
fortunes of Mr. Worsdale's family, " in whom," as she
had said in an extremely well-written letter to Mrs.
Sherwin, " she must always feel a tender interest;"
and I daresay would not have been averse to a
renewal of intimacy in that quarter; but as Dolly

had not responded with any degree of cordiality, Miss Skimple was too well-bred, and certainly too sagacious, to venture further. However, while at Tonbridge Wells she casually met with a charming young person, the daughter of an esteemed Christian friend, who had recently been united to the worthy and energetic Rector of Heron's Mount, and gladly accepted a pressing invitation to stay a few weeks at the Rectory.

She had been much charmed, she wrote to say, with the visit; the Rectory was a model of a Christian home, she told me, and that Mrs. Palethorpe, whom her husband affectionately called "Tiny," was a ray of sunshine wherever she appeared. She had been also much impressed by the zeal and the unostentatious charity of the worthy Rector; even at dinner, before serving his wife or his guest, he would select the choicest morsel of the dish for one of his poor parishioners, who might be tempted by the delicacy; and more than once had left them at the table, that he might himself have the unselfish delight of witnessing the poor creature's grateful emotion.

I learnt also that, a few months after the marriage, Mrs. Dingwall had presented herself at the Rectory, with the manifest intention of making a lengthened sojourn, stating that as she didn't know what might happen, she had thought it better to be near her dear daughter.

But as nothing did happen, and as the dear daughter did not agree very well with her anxious mamma, the perfect picture of a Christian home became slightly indistinct, so that an on-looker might have had some difficulty in recognising the Rectory by Miss Skimple's description; especially as the " ray of sunshine" during Mrs. Dingwall's visit was very like those intermittent beams we obtain in December or January, the glimpse of which only serves to make us regret the more their prolonged absence. I believe, after the good lady had taken a tearful departure for Congleton, the Rectory resumed its wonted aspect. Not having any family to engross her attention, Martha was able to devote a great portion of her time to the composition of serious works adapted for the reading of the young—or of pleasant narratives, ever written with an object, though fictitious. The instructive treatise, " Who shall deliver me ?" and the touching verses, " When blindly in the dark I wander," were the emanations of her thoughtful pen, and commanded an extensive sale ; indeed, the pleasing melody to which the words of the verses were set, was the work of the Reverend Ernest himself, and used to be sung by the school children with much effect.

The last time I saw the worthy Rector he had grown very stout, and the last I heard of him was after his elevation to the bench as a justice of the peace. He had attracted some public attention in that capacity by one or two judgments he had delivered, notably in connexion with the punishment awarded in the case of a child of tender years, who had been charged with the theft of an apple or two from one of the Rectory trees that hung over the highway; and it was no doubt in consideration of his many duties in the parish, and with a thoughtful regard for his health, that the Lord Chancellor had kindly proposed to relieve him of his additional responsibilities, and had invited him to retire from the judicial bench, which I am told he in consequence did.

I do not think I have ever seen Frank Ossett for half an hour, that our conversation has not turned on our old Dalesford acquaintance, and the times and scenes I have endeavoured to narrate. I believe he remained a bachelor, solely because he never entirely overcame his boyish love for Miss Dolly—though he never confessed it; but replied to all questions tending in that direction, that he supposed he was not a marrying man, and could not settle down, on which I have my own opinion. Certainly he remained on the best of terms with his friends, though he confided his opinion to me on one occasion, that Mr. Sherwin, when he condescended to the masquerade of a foreman of a factory, was adopting an unworthy course of deception, and had thus brought on himself and on poor little Dolly many of the troubles they subsequently had to endure; and that, after all, it was only a scheme that an egotistical and suspicious nature would have conceived. I do not know but Mr. Frank was right; and I admit as well, that Dolly herself, in that rebellious spirit which she occasionally displayed, inherited no doubt from her resolute old father, was not that perfect young person we expect to find in the heroine of a story like this. But I daresay Frank liked her none the less for that; and, indeed, I am inclined to the opinion that as a rule, we love the best those characters of which the failings are occasionally visible, as the most perfect form on the painter's canvas or in the sculptor's marble, is less attractive than the real flesh and blood, that speaks and moves, but is not created according to the rigid lines and rules of classic beauty.

Perhaps the character of each—with the flaws and foibles it may have possessed—was sufficiently well known to the other, that such defects but rarely appeared; and so Joe and Dolly travelled the journey of life together, side by side, happy in their well-tried affection, and conscientiously discharging the duties of the position in which Providence had graciously placed them. The very independence of Joe's character, and his habit of self-control, which sometimes approached reserve, may have narrowed his circle of acquaintance, though I question if it estranged his friends; and although not a popular man in his native town, no one was more deeply or generally respected. It was for Dolly that the esteem was intensified by the love her character inspired. It was her gentle voice that whispered the words of hope or sympathy, and her light hand that smoothed the pillow of pain and misery, or ministered to suffering with the tenderness and delicacy that belonged to her.

I have finished my story of this little Yorkshire family. If I have fallen into the errors of certain historians and biographers, and coloured some of my characters with the tints most pleasant to my own eyes, the outlines of the forms at least were already drawn to my hand, and I have merely arranged in groups for contrast or harmony the individual figures as I found them.

I submit, we often seek in the pages of fiction for stirring incidents or romantic character, when, in truth, they are on all sides of us, if we would but take trouble or exercise sagacity in the search for them; as the native of California or Australia, probably, barters the necessaries of life for a glass bead or a piece of Birmingham jewellery, though beneath his foot may lurk a mine of precious metal, only awaiting the enterprise of the intelligent observer to be developed. For, wherever the strong human heart beats vigorously and the active brain of man is at work, there will always be the fierce passions and the tender sympathy, the reckless daring and the calm endurance, the persistent knavery and the simple honesty, the truth and purity, vice and falsehood, that make up the heroism or the romance of life.

Thus, like the driver of the old-fashioned stage conveyance, I have picked up my passengers by the wayside, simply as I have met them; and, having left them at their several places of destination, until I have parted with them all, I come to the termination of my journey—and so ends my story.

THE END.